Love in a Nutbag

To gorgeous + wonderful Emma
— may your life be filled with lots of nutbag moments —
Love Lisa

Love in a Nutbag

Lisa Ammerman

Writers Club Press
San Jose New York Lincoln Shanghai

Love in a Nutbag

Writers Club Press
an imprint of iUniverse.com, Inc.

For information address:
iUniverse.com, Inc.
5220 S 16th, Ste. 200
Lincoln, NE 68512
www.iuniverse.com

This book is a work of fiction. Names, characters and places are products of the author's imagination. Any resemblance is entirely coincidental.

Cover by Julia Turk: "Universe"—*Navigators Tarot of the Mystic Sea*

ISBN: 0-595-19719-1

Printed in the United States of America

For Big Grandma

Lovers don't finally meet somewhere.
They're in each other all along.

—Rumi

Foreword

Love in a Nutbag is a novel I'm confident will have a significant appeal for readers who enjoy novels that present a combination of literary, intellectual as well as sexual and romantic interest.

The story presents a "parallel montage" in the lives of two women—the modern granddaughter and the dead grandmother, suggesting how the two lives are bound together in a common quest for those epiphanies, or moments of intense (often sexual) fulfillment, that come out of the "nutbag" that our otherwise humdrum and prosaic lives occasionally present to us. In a nutshell (!), the story, while rooted in real life, presents a subtle line between easy-read and soft-core literary with a sprinkle of sexual realism. Though I am not a woman, I personally found the novel enjoyable and compulsive reading, so it may well have a wider appeal; and while it may well cater for the romantic inclination of the Joanna Trollope reader, it will, as I said, certainly appeal to the 'thinking' woman—and man! It has energy and emotional texture as well as beautifully crafted language. The style is succinct, the language evocative—both sensuous and sensual.

Charles Muller, MA (Wales), PhD (London), DLitt (OFS), DEd (SA)

Chapter One

Becky

My grandmother had this little ritual. I think it started when I was about eight years old. As far as I can remember, and for some reason (known only to her) she decided age eight was the right time to begin.

The ritual was something new and I guess I can't really call it spooky, but for some reason I've never been able to remember much of anything else about my childhood. Not with such certainty, or knack for detail. As to why my grandmother wanted me—in particular—to take part, that's anyone's guess. Except I, Nina Dawson, was her only granddaughter. All her other grandchildren were boys. So perhaps in that sense her special attention was justified.

On the day this little ritual started—I was eating lunch. Not just any lunch, mind you, but the one I liked best: hamburger patties, cheese macaroni, corn pudding, biscuits with gravy. My grandma put sugar in her corn pudding, making it extra sweet; her gravy was generously salted and thick with lumps. I liked mashing the lumps, smearing them over my biscuits with a spoon. And although my mother often served instant macaroni, grandma's squishy cheddar pasta always tasted better.

"Don't forget the limas," my grandmother insisted, smiling as she handed me the bowl.

Admittedly, I'd normally dismiss pale-green beans slumped in a sea of tomato sauce as disgusting—but I'd always end up eating them.

You see, my grandmother lived in the hills of Central Pennsylvania where the mountain air makes you really hungry.

Of course, my favorite lunch (aside from the limas) was served up and devoured by the entire family. But in fact it was a preparation: a sign meant just for me. For after I turned eight, whenever my grandmother served this same menu, she'd decide to leave the washing up to my mother—declaring her digestion wasn't like it used to be, which I suspect was an excuse.

"The best thing for it is a walk," she'd insist, rubbing her stomach. Then: "Fancy coming with me, Nina?"

The first time she asked I didn't feel very inclined to go.

But seeing me shake my head, my grandmother smiled and muttered, "Oh, well, I just thought you might like to meet my special friends, in the woods." That did it. I knew she meant the deer, and I was dying to see some. For although our grandma's house sat right next to the woods, my brothers and I were never allowed to go looking for them on our own.

I have to admit I never *did* see any deer, but for years my grandmother and I carried on with the ritual: first I'd eat my favorite lunch, then I'd follow her out the back door and we'd climb up the hill together, weaving through a vast, eerie maze of thick evergreen.

She would lead me deep into the woods, stopping occasionally for a rest. Whenever I got impatient, she'd always find some deer droppings to keep up my interest. And then, after a long hush, when we'd given up trying to spot our friends camouflaged in the surrounding bark, she would suddenly whisper: "You are a very special girl, Nina, and I love you very, very much."

These words, and her voice so full of emotion, never failed to send a hot tingle down my spine. I could see how she was trying to show me something through the tears in her eyes, and I wondered what it meant.

The next whisper, too, was always the same: "When I'm gone, Nina, I want you to have this." Then she'd hold out her hand and show me her ring.

I'll never forget that first time with the ring—because I didn't want to look at it. No, I looked into my grandma's eyes instead, and what I saw there was a bit of a shock. Those weren't my grandma's eyes: they'd changed into something quite different—like an ocean far, far away and so deep nobody would ever know just how far down it went, let alone ever reach the bottom.

When I saw her eyes looking like that I felt uneasy. Uncomfortable. But she didn't seem to mind. She was more concerned over how I felt about the ring.

"Nina, I want to show you something."

She would repeat this, lowering her arm with its soft freckled wrinkles of flesh sagging straight out—angled just so—in front of my face. I noticed how her thin, bony fingers trembled. Then, suddenly, the fingers splayed apart—rigid—like the ribs of an umbrella opening, and the ring would catch a passing shift of sunlight, breaking through the evergreens.

"Oh!" A sparkle would shoot out, the beam flashing across my face.

The next second it would be gone.

Then, with her other hand clutching the collar of her blouse (as if to steady herself), my grandma waited while I stared at the ring for what I considered to be a sufficient amount of time. As far as rings go, I thought it was very nice: a large round diamond surrounded by eight tiny blue sapphires, shaped like a flower.

But of course I wasn't very interested at that age. What really mattered was the way she'd started to look at me—with those eyes.

"It's a pretty ring, grandma," I'd say. But I remember I didn't like the way it made her eyes look. I kept thinking I'd never be able to stare at them again for very long. Short snatches were all right; broken glances from face to shoulder or wall beyond, but never a real good look.

Why not? What was happening in her eyes? At the time I didn't know—being eight years old. I only felt a child's fear of somehow going where it wasn't safe or permitted. Then wishing I hadn't, like slipping open my parents' bedroom door, curious, when I should have been asleep.

And my grandmother kept making a ritual out of showing me this ring, the once or twice a year when my parents brought us to visit. It was as if she'd never done it before. Nine, ten, eleven, twelve years old. I'd be led into the woods and told "when I'm gone, you'll have this" dozens of times. Each time she'd remind me, show me the ring; while as I grew older, her fingers seemed to grow smaller, slimmer, more wrinkled; but the ring was always the same.

I can still see them today. My grandmother's strange eyes, and behind my parent's door, too: moist, naked images lying exposed and yet at the same time so untouchable. Go further—look beyond—and enter a dark and mysterious place. Wordless. A world beyond words. All humping and sighing.

So I'd close my eyes and let my grandmother hold me tight for a minute. She'd show me the ring, then bend down and hug me.

"It makes me so happy, to know that some day this will be yours," she'd mumble, before letting go.

"I know," I'd say. That was all I could muster. "I know, Grandma."

But it took me a long time to know—not until much later—that she wasn't really talking about the ring.

*

In the beginning my grandmother, Becky Callum, lived in the central mountains of Pennsylvania. She was born in 1908, in a mining town called Philipsburg. When she was five, her father, a miner, was killed in a pit accident—so she and her four sisters where brought up by her mother and grandmother. Her mother's family helped support them, but it was a struggle to keep food on the table and coal in the stove.

Becky grew up determined to better herself. Having a stubborn nature and a quick mind, she convinced her mother to let her attend school, while her other sisters stayed home earning their living by sewing and mending other people's clothes.

Becky wasn't very pretty, but being so absorbed in her learning, she didn't much care. She was almost six feet tall (too tall for a girl), with a hard, rugged look about her features. Her square-shaped face was accentuated by a long nose curiously matched by a set of pinched, upturned nostrils. Her lips were soft and plump, but too small in proportion to the wide face. With long, gangling legs and not much of a waist, she wasn't the epitome of feminine beauty. But she did have two arresting features: big brown eyes and larger-than-average breasts.

The breasts, of course, were kept hidden. And her eyes were always buried behind books. So instead of getting herself pregnant in her teens (like most girls in the backwoods of Pennsylvania), Becky Callum graduated High School first in her class. First in a class of sixty-two.

She was presented a scholarship, to study English Literature at Penn University. In those days, a scholarship was a rare opportunity for a penniless young woman from Philipsburg to better herself. Now she could become a librarian, or maybe even a teacher; she could leave the black filth of a coal town with its depressed shanties and uncivilized mountain forests for the clean, high cultured, spanking-white clapboard shores of Philadelphia.

But events were to take an unexpected turn for Becky.

I always held my breath at this point in the story.

I'd heard it a few times before, when I'd managed to summon up the courage to ask her. But of course the ending never made much sense—not until I had a few brushes with the nutbag myself.

The nutbag, you see, is a mystery. Something to solve, from beginning to end. And like a detective, for the past twelve years I've been trying to fill in the gaps.

"So Grandma, why didn't you ever go to college?"

"Nina, I told you already. I met your grandfather."

"Tell me again."

In my early teens I persisted in asking questions my grandmother only half answered. But even then I knew she wasn't telling all of it—because of her eyes.

I suspected there were parts of the story that went much deeper than words: how she'd met my grandfather, and what happened after that was all a big mistake. She didn't have to tell me so, for someone like me to know. You see my grandfather was a fine man, but he didn't have eyes like Becky's. That's all there was to go on, you see...my first little snippet of truth.

*

Becky was seventeen when she graduated high school. It was June, 1926 when she set off for the Dawson's dairy farm to deliver some mended socks. Mr. Dawson's wife had died last year so they had no women folk to do such work. Becky carried the socks in a large basket which would hold the milk and eggs Mr. Dawson would give her in return.

It was just after sunset, and the grackles were rustling for position in the row of ash trees that bordered the road. Becky was halfway there. Just past the trees with the noisy grackles, she could see the farm in the distance, sitting on a barren, tree-felled hill with the dense, forested mountains looming behind. Her heavy walking boots stumbled over large chunks of wagon dirt, rock-hard from the lack of rain. Still another mile to go.

But she didn't mind. She enjoyed the solitude, the green fields and grazing cows, the wild flowers and tall grass, the cool shade and silence of the surrounding woods. She loved the smell of evergreen and the prickle of pine.

Yet evening was closing in; so now, brushing a swirling cloud of gnats from her face, she quickened her stride. The sun had already disappeared over the mountain and the soft folds of shadow creeping down toward the valley would soon turn dark—then black, as nights in the Pennsylvania mountains were always the blackest of black.

At a much faster pace Becky climbed the hill and passed through the outer gate, heading up the track to the old house. The place looked sad. Tired. The bright yellow paint on the clapboard siding had vanished long ago, leaving long splintered strips of peeling white undercoat and bare wood.

Becky imagined the house in it's original glory as she approached: all lemon and smooth and gleaming, with dark-green window shutters, and a white porch. But she stopped her daydreaming as soon as she spotted one of Mr. Dawson's sons, Clem, standing near the barn.

Clem, a tall, robust lad with thick brown hair and plump, pouty lips, didn't see her—he was too busy struggling with his horse. The horse seemed stubborn and apparently didn't like being hitched to a wagon. The wagon, just visible in the dark recess of the barn, jolted in and out of the doorway each time the horse bolted.

Becky walked by, pausing to watch the scene and smile at poor Clem—who, preoccupied as he was, still sensed her presence and managed to turn and smile back. Meanwhile the wagon kept jolting and the horse kept jumping at each thrust of Clem's arm, as he tried to clip the bit.

Was it the warm June air, or the memory of *Paradise Lost* she'd just finished reading the night before, or the flush of youth still fresh in her veins? Whatever it was, Becky stopped dead in her tracks. She simply stood—transfixed—and stared at Clem. And for the first time she felt a deep longing for something RAW. As raw and fleshy as the smooth, firm muscles on Clem's arms.

That's when it happened: Becky's eyes started to see raw. She didn't know how else she might describe it: like catching a piece of heaven, unawares, in the buff. Raw. Stripped bare, so every little detail comes alive before her eyes, and has a life of its own. Strange...how Clem and the horse could be the most amazing and beautiful sight she'd ever seen. Those very arms, sweating and bulging as they heaved and pulled the reins tight; and then, with an exhilarating ease, even tighter. Those worn and creased leather boots, planted firmly in a ball of dust and grinding even more dust upwards; up to his thighs and mingling round the twist and turn of his waist.

How divine! Even the dust. At that moment she longed to become the dust; to dance unseen round his boots, invisibly licking the raw secret. To get that close!

But instead she had to keep her distance: eyes resting on the boots, the legs, the crotch, the chest, the throat, the sweat, the hands, the rough, vein-lined, pulsating, taut and rippling brown-skinned, sun-tanned muscles of Clem.

Becky's eyes feasted on the raw, bare strength of the man and the earth that made him so. She stared like no decent woman should, let alone be thinking such thoughts.

So at the same time she had to turn away, before Clem might notice. Squeezing her eyes shut for a moment, and pulling the basket up even higher, she resumed her march—in a slow daze—toward the house.

But she felt strange and different. Not only were her eyes seeing raw, but her legs felt wobbly. And this other Becky had private parts that felt strange and different, too. Moist. Throbbing with a deep, searing ache.

"Tell your mother thank you, 'n all, and John's gettin' married come August, too." Mr. Dawson's third son, Ben, wrapped the eggs in a towel and carefully stuffed them inside the basket with the milk.

"To Rachel?" Becky asked, letting him arrange the eggs but thinking she should be doing it herself. Though she couldn't concentrate; not now, not inside the house, talking to Ben. It felt like a dream—her mind and body still standing back there, transfixed, in front of the barn.

"Yep, and he'll be needin' a new shirt," said Ben. "There'll be more mendin' too, sure."

"But nothing now," she added.

"Nope. Sorry."

Becky nodded, not caring whether there was more mending or not. Hadn't her sisters asked her to mention Rachel's first-born soon on the way? Suggest a baby blanket trimmed in lace? Wouldn't the Dawsons be needing a baby blanket in addition to the wedding shirt? But she didn't say any of it. Instead, she bent down to stroke the backs of three little kittens frantically rubbing her ankles. Amazing: the soft, wispy fur on these kittens. One ginger, one gray, one black. Soft like velvet, with warm, delicate throats purring like mad.

She felt better simply stroking the kittens and saying nothing.

The farm had many, many cats. Soon they'd be treated like vermin, Becky was thinking. Soon they'd have a new mistress—the young bride Rachel. She'd have them all put outside. Clean up the mess. A woman wouldn't stand for it, a strong acid smell when you walked in the door.

While Becky, experiencing a cat in the raw, couldn't imagine why. All she felt was this seductive fur, as smooth as silk; a coat warmer than a wool blanket, and the subtle vibration of purring as she stroked it.

Yet even so, stepping outside again, Becky was glad to breathe the fresh air. The kittens and several older cats chased behind her, shooting past her feet. They scattered across the front doorstep; disappeared under the porch.

But Clem was still there, waiting by the barn—with the wagon. The dust had settled; the horse had given in.

He waved. Becky could feel her heart pounding. Of course she could have a ride back to town, if he was going there himself on some errand. But seeing and feeling as she did that moment—she hesitated.

"Come on, it's gettin' too dark to walk now," Clem insisted, as if anticipating her answer.

Becky nodded. When she got to the wagon he helped her up.

*

"When I first met your grandfather, he was still working on his father's farm," my grandmother said. This was what she said. "He gave me a ride in his wagon one day, and we started courting after that."

"So you both fell in love at first sight?"

"I suppose so, but in those days you didn't talk like that. We didn't discuss such subjects."

"Such subjects? Then what did you talk about?"

"The farm, the weather, the church bazaar, the marriage of John and Rachel, the health of his father, my mother..."

All lies. They didn't talk, not on that wagon the first time Becky saw Clem as a man. I'm sure of that by the way she spoke, and twisted that ring around and around on her finger. Hiding the truth in her eyes.

In her eyes, his hands held the reins, sleeves rolled back, arms tense in vein-muscled grip. His body rocked against hers, as the wagon swayed, and she wasn't looking at the fields, or the trees, or the hard clumps of dirt on the road. She was looking at flesh and blood: the easy rhythm of his thighs, set firmly apart, and the way his legs swept down into his boots, propped against the wooden sideboard.

She tried to stop seeing raw by looking at his face—a quick glance that was all—but no, that didn't help. It didn't help, his stubbly jaw and lips slightly open, half-smiling in a knowing way. His eyes squinting intently at the horse and his muttering, "Hey boy, that's it," in a soft chuckling sound between his teeth.

She could think of nothing else to do.

"I'll walk now, please!" she said, suddenly. Blurted out with it. The only words spoken, out of nowhere.

It was quite dark by then, maybe a mile out of town. Clem didn't say a word—not even in protest. And if only he had said something! If only he, or she, had found words to speak, that unbearable unspeakable feeling might have gone away.

But something else happened. Did Clem know? Had he seen behind her eyes? She was wondering this, while the wagon bumped along and still—silence.

"I said I'll walk now."

It seemed to take ages, but finally the horse's head pulled back; the wheels slowed to a halt. Clem draped the reins over his thighs and sat still for a minute—arms rigid at his sides. Then he turned to Becky. He looked at her as if they'd both been having a very pleasurable conversation together and she decided to end it for no good reason. And he knew perfectly well that she was enjoying it just as much as he was—if not more.

Then his eyes traveled down the line of shiny black buttons that ran from the neck of her gray cotton dress, to her lap, and along the creases of cloth draped down to her ankles. Lingered there.

And like a ghost, or demon, two hands suddenly sprang out of the darkness and grabbed her waist, wordlessly; hands circling round tight and pulling her to the side of the wagon.

Becky grabbed something—Clem's neck—as she felt herself being pressed against him. As they both slumped down from the wagon into the road, she saw Clem throw her a look telling her to say stop, stop now if she would have him stop. But she wanted to know, not stop: to know how the unspeakable feeling works between two strangers who thrust aside words, and clinging together, throw themselves into the tall grass.

Yes, the hands she watched harness the horse now groped to catch her own body and it wasn't a dream. She was lying in the grass, Clem moving his head downwards, slowly passing his lips across the buttons of her dress. She could no longer see his face—only feel his hands gently pulling her clothing up. She didn't look but she could feel her skirt moving up, inch by inch, very slowly, until it stopped.

She didn't move. Not even as she felt her skirt at her waist, her underclothes being pushed aside, and cool lips pressing against the soft white cotton around her crotch—then skin—

Clem's head buried below, pressing against her sex, her pulsating secret. Holding it there, there, there.

Holding.

"But why didn't you speak? Why couldn't you explain it, Grandma?" This was what I wanted to ask her.

I persisted in wondering about the truth—but not until much later, when I was in High School. By then I'd finally begun to understand why my grandma had that look in her eyes, only she couldn't answer. She was dead. The only tangible thing left was the ring.

Lying in the grass with a man pressing his head…

You see, I know the true story of the wagon. I caught a glimpse of what really happened. At least I think I did. For when I was still quite young, maybe twelve years old, and my grandma said "he gave me a ride on his wagon one day," the scene just popped into my head. I remember staring at my grandmother and feeling this urge to close my eyes. So I did. I closed my eyes and suddenly in the darkness I was pushing aside a curtain, and then finding myself past the darkness—into the light. But the light was dim, like the beginning of night, and it was me, sitting on the wagon with Clem. Just like Becky. Then I was falling off, falling into a man's arms and feeling the grass cushion my body as this man's lips, his hands, moved over me.

That's what happened: the curtain opened and with my eyes closed, I caught the scene as clear as can be, just as if I was right there on the stage myself.

Of course I could be wrong, but why would I have conjured up a scene like that in my head, as a young girl? Would my childish imagination create something only an adult could understand? And ever since, that wagon of hers has niggled, like an obvious clue.

But the curtain won't open again—no matter how hard I close my eyes and will it to.

So what went wrong after the wagon? Something went wrong. Only my grandmother never said, and I wanted an answer.

And I wondered too, why didn't she ever speak to me about such things? Warn me? Explain about the different kinds of passion?

Maybe she knew it was something I had to find out for myself. For I still get the feeling she gave me her ring hoping I might carry on—without making the same mistake.

So that's where it begins, I think. Having the kind of eyes that see behind. Going as deep as raw secrets.

And I bet if Becky could hear me now she wouldn't titter back and say, "So, Nina, what exactly do you mean by a nutbag? A packet of peanuts—or a mixed jumble of pecans, almonds and cashews?"

Chapter Two

The Nutbag

Now. It's 1977, exactly fifty years since my grandmother gave birth to my dad. I'm twenty-one years old, and still trying to get past the wagon.

I'm not even sure how to explain the nutbag.

Which makes me wonder if that's why my grandmother never mentioned it herself.

But somebody should, I'm thinking. Not that the "mystery of the nutbag" is the perfect phrase for it, but it's the best I can do.

So to begin, I'm pretty much like everybody else.

I exist. Only I have to admit that for most of the time, I don't really feel like I'm existing. Not really.

It's no big deal, I suppose. But why not? What is or isn't a big deal? I only know what I feel. And I don't feel alive—really alive—unless a particular kind of heaven hits me. When that happens it's all right: being alive makes some sense and that's got to be a big deal.

It does happen sometimes. Not only do I know I exist, but I'm inflame, aflame, a fame, a crazy glowing star, a beacon of the universe.

One of those moments when I'm convinced I'm the star of an Oscar-winning movie, and there's a judging panel that's been keeping tabs all along and handing out trophies.

Sometimes. But most of the time it's just a goddamned dream.

I guess most of the time it's bullshit, so I go about my business just like everybody else: your ordinary person doing the ordinary things everybody else does.

So I'm sitting here in Building 2C, Room 706, at UCLA—listening to a lecture. In the last row, and so far back and high up I can barely hear the professor's words.

But it doesn't matter. I'm not really listening.

To what? Well, something is being said about the course textbook's theory of finance and inflation. Hands go up, several students voice their particular concerns. I nod, look concerned too, but I'm more worried about whether or not I'm feeling alive. Though half a point interest rate going up or down at the right time might make a big difference. Or so they say.

No, I'm not completely oblivious. In fact, a freckled, frizzy-haired boy three rows down is standing up…and I notice how his views are taken. A wave of muffled grunts and chuckles cuts through the somber air. I do hear that—even the subtle murmur of movement, of shaking heads. No, no, young man, you got it all wrong. Which makes me feel sorry. Like him.

Who's being stupid? It's me, I'm thinking. Me. Nina Dawson. I should have owned up and registered as a Philosophy major. But it's too late now, I'm already a senior. Guess I hoped Economics might force me to fit in.

Fit in? Jesus, and who am I fooling now? A few statistics. Possibly a handful of strangers.

The freckled boy sits down. Sits again, blushing. Probably wishes he could bury his head in his notebook.

I watch him for a minute, wonder how to explain.

I could tell him the story of the nutbag, part of me is thinking. You know, explain. He might feel better. The whole story? Yes. And why not? Because it's scary. He might think I'm missing a few marbles. Or got too many marbles for my own good. And Jesus, none of this is about marbles.

No, I'm not sure whether to tell him or simply keep my mouth shut. It probably wouldn't be so hard if I didn't know about the other thing—the thing behind the flame. But I do, and being just an ordinary person, with a practical-minded major, I have trouble finding other people who know what I mean.

"What are you on?" I get asked.

Just as an example, people ask me this a lot. "What are you on?"

I'm hoping this is a joke. But apparently it's not, so I think about it for a minute and say, "The seat of my chair."

Because I'm not that sure what I'm on. I often wonder how I got this way, and who or what I could blame. I suppose if I think hard enough, I could name names, point out places, suggest possible answers. But even if it makes sense, it never changes anything.

The only thing I do know for certain is that when I'm really existing the flame flickers. Sometimes it flickers, and believe it if you will, this world of shit actually dumps heaven on me.

So instead of answering the question "What are you on?" with my usual standby, "the seat of my chair," I'm thinking, well, I could say something else. I could say I'm pretty sure "I'm on" what I call a nutbag. That's it, I guess: a bag of nuts. I wait around, pretending to exist, until the nutbag appears again (which it always does), as if quite on purpose, to dump yet another nugget on my head.

One of those moments that suddenly hit you from out of the blue where you're feeling so good you can't stop smiling and thanking god you're alive.

I've chewed these nuts, you see, and the taste is pretty good. No, I mean too good. So I'm either "on" the trail of the nutbag or remembering how it felt the last time it appeared. Just to bring back the feeling again. The sensation itself is as real and distinct as the claws of a cat, or the throb of an orgasm.

So if it isn't a nutbag, well, as far as I'm concerned—it's got to be scuzz. The dirt, dust or scum that grows and collects on everything, including a nutbag, and you name it.

Shit. So there's only one prayer for the likes of me. Just one.

But now the lecture's over. Time to stop thinking, and blink as the lights go back on. That's it: ears bombarded with the roar of clapping, legs jostled by fellow students brushing past, I stuff the notebook into my bag, stand up, stretch my legs, follow the crowd weaving out like a herd of dazed cattle. My body bumping, pressing forward. Onward to the next pasture.

I move on, sometimes on tip-toe, scanning the bobbing line of heads to see if I can spot the freckled boy. But his frizzy mop is nowhere to be seen. Oh well. What next?

Now I'm smiling to myself, because if I'm sure about anything, I'm sure about this: all I have to do is keep wiping the scuzz off my nutbag, that's all. And wait for the answer to come.

Chapter Three

Nina

It was the summer of 1970 when I met Robby Alfonsio and things started to happen. We were living in Maryland by then.

I was fourteen and my parents were beginning to annoy me. Especially my father. For as it happened, Becky's first child, Andrew, grew up to become my dad. So in a way he was part of the cause-and-effect of the wagon experience.

But my dad never blamed grandma's ritual with the ring. He had theories of his own. I mean, when he tried to figure out what it was I "was on" and how he could get me off it.

"Nina, you're way too young," he'd insist, "to be reading what you're reading."

"No I'm not," I'd answer, nevertheless closing the book of whatever I happened to have open. I did feel a bit guilty. Soaking up passion from the "fiction classics" section of the local bookstore wasn't the norm for a fourteen year old. Not if it wasn't part of one's English assignment.

Nevertheless, I had just finished *The Idiot*, *War and Peace*, *Lolita*, and *Tess of the D'Urbervilles*. Even worse, but fortunately unbeknown to my dad, I had grabbed a book off the philosophy shelves, Sartre's *Being and Nothingness*. Though I'd only managed to get as far as the third chapter.

My dad didn't think it was healthy, reading so many books.

"You're supposed to be interested in things like records, lipstick and boys!"

"Oh, you mean, like Led Zeppelin so you can scream at me to turn it down?" I quipped. "Or black mascara, red lipstick and blue eye shadow so you shout at me to take it off?"

My dad didn't seem amused. "And boys?"

"I'm into boys," I answered. But before he could look too relieved, I added, "though you'll have to save that lecture on the dangers of petting for later. Right now I'm crazy about older men. Guys who, even if I wanted them to, wouldn't touch me."

"I wouldn't be too sure of that," he mumbled.

The thought still made me blush. "I'm definitely in love with Sidney Carton," I confessed.

"Who?"

"—and the Scarlet Pimpernel, and Heathcliff, and the Reverend Dimmsdale…"

"I'm not saying you shouldn't read—just not so much," he pleaded, interrupting. "You're too smart, and good-looking, to shut yourself away in your room, head buried in your books most of the time."

"You think I'm copping out?" I could feel my voice begin to shake. I hated this sort of thing. But he never gave up, pestering me with his incessant know-it-all, go-get-em attitude.

"Well, yes. Why don't you ever *do* anything? Get yourself out and about more, like other kids your age? Try out for cheerleading squad. Join a bowling team. Have a few girlfriends over, once in a while…"

"Because it's not *me*!" I insisted. Then, before he could see me burst into tears, I rushed (with my book) upstairs.

Strewn across my bed I would say the things I had really wanted to say—into the pillow. Things like "Who's copping out? Who's *really* copping out? No dad, it's not me. I'm going for it, going for the kind of *life* I want to find—and it's in books. I'm reading to meet new people all the time; people who have a *soul*, who feel *passion*. I'm putting myself in a world where I fit in. Sorry, but I don't feel comfortable anywhere else. It's not that I haven't tried. I have. Is it my fault there's nobody around with my kind of eyes in the whole of Calverton Junior High?"

By then I was aware of the signposts, lurking in eyes. And without really realizing it, I started lusting after the nut. My first nut, mine and mine alone, to bag.

True, my father must have inherited his mother's brains. He had a knack for mathematics and physics. By the time he was ten years old, he had already decided he wanted to be a mathematics teacher. He breezed through college, then postgraduate school, and wound up a Physics professor.

Pennsylvania wasn't highbrow enough for my dad. So he accepted a teaching position near Washington DC. That's why we left Philadelphia two years earlier and moved to Gaithersburg, Maryland. Needless to say, my father was the only one who had really wanted to go. My mom, brothers and I weren't too happy about it. My grandmother cried her eyes out, of course, the last day we saw her before we left. But after a few months everybody, including poor old grandma, got used to it.

Gaithersburg was all right. At least it couldn't be lumped in with sprawling suburbs of DC. Eighty miles to the west, and well off the freeway, it was still "out in the country" even though most of the land was obviously on the brink of development. The farms, fields and roadsides all bore the signs: lines of sticks with plastic red flags flanked the fences; crater-sized holes surrounded the outskirts of town; new tarmac roads began and ended abruptly, billboards boasting "Coming Soon!"

But nothing really substantial had been built quite yet. Just one small-scale Mall next to Safeway, which was convenient in winter. Plus, here and there, an 'experimental' patch of new homes recently constructed on fields too hilly and barren to be much good for anything else. And finally, with great forethought and specifically to lure in more families like us, an impressive new High School and Junior High had just opened last fall. Both schools were sprawling brick edifices: modern, efficient, surrounded by turfed playing fields, lighted tennis courts, and a cement grandstand around the stadium.

So my parents chose Gaithersburg. I went to the new Junior High. My brother Jeff, who was sixteen, had the privilege of attending the High School. Our baby brother, Teddy, who was only seven, had to settle for the decrepit-looking elementary school.

Our house was a large brick affair, a two-story with four bedrooms and detached garage. It sat on Oakhill Road, a new residential block built over a hill with a nice view of the open countryside. There weren't any oaks around, but at the bottom of the hill, past the barbed wire fence, a small wooded area of mixed trees (mostly ash and birch) wound its way along a creek running between more hills. About a mile away you could see a few farm buildings nestled along the edge of the trees and creek.

My brothers and I knew every nook and cranny of that creek. Up to the point where it reached the farm, that is. We also knew by name every family member living in each and every house in the Oakhill Road circle. There were twenty homes in all, and since our little colony was stuck in the middle of nowhere—like a marooned patch of civilization on Mars—we all stuck together.

Anyway, it was in the summer of 1970, when I was fourteen, that my dad decided I wasn't turning out to be the kind of daughter he'd had in mind. It was getting pretty obvious, how I wasn't going to grow out of it. Adolescence meant letting go of my silly childhood fancies, or, as my father liked to put it, "Nina's secret fairyland." I guess my dad, like Clem, was a practical man at heart.

So finally, as a consequence, and in order to please him (as my mother never seemed to concern herself over such matters), I decided to *do* something. Act normal. Put down my books. Throw myself into something tangible, like socializing or sports.

I considered the options, and girlie pursuits were definitely out. For one thing, I didn't think I was very good-looking. Meaning my dad was wrong, or at best, rather biased. And it's hard to play the girlie game when you don't have the proper equipment. Honestly, my complexion was too ruddy and acne-prone to be dabbling in make-up. My hair—dull brown, thick and frizzy—made a complete mockery of curlers. And to top it off, I just couldn't wear mini-skirts or go-go boots because I didn't have the figure. No such luck, taking after my mother, who was gorgeous. Instead, I was cursed with the hefty Callum physique: big bones, broad chest, wide waist, and legs shaped like extra-long Cuban cigars.

But even if I did have the equipment, or fudged it, I knew I'd never score in the personality department. Of course other girls can do it—by being flirty, chatty, giggly, or downright pushy. But what if you've got lips so stubborn to open, you'd have to walk around carrying a wrench?

So thinking it all over, I went for sports. And the following afternoon after school, I announced to my brother Jeff I wanted to play baseball.

"But you can't throw!" he exclaimed.

"Then I'll be an outfielder. I could play right field. I can catch."

Jeff shook his head.

"Come on Jeff, *other* girls play. Patty and Deb are allowed to play, aren't they? I've seen Betsy out there too. She can't throw any further than me."

Every afternoon during the summer a group of kids from the neighborhood would show up at the vacant lot between the Morrison's and Babcock's for a game of baseball. My brother Jeff, being the oldest, was automatically a team captain. The other captain usually turned out to be Robert Alfonsio, who was also sixteen. But he didn't always show.

I had occasionally watched them play, for a few minutes, from my bedroom window. The front end of the lot was just visible from my room—across the street, four houses down to the left. Once in awhile I'd look up from my book when there was a particularly loud *crack* and the yells and screams grew louder. I'd hear it and glance out the window to catch Johnny or Patty (who also couldn't throw) misjudge the distance of the fly ball and end up running backwards—furiously—across the flowerbed on the Morrison's front lawn.

I would smile to myself whenever this happened, which meant the neighborhood game of baseball was, after all, amusing. And to be one of few girls who dared to swing a bat and wield a mitt along with the boys...well...that was even better. My dad would love it. Besides, it was true: I *could* catch.

"Hey Nina, comin' to play?"

"Yep."

"You are?"

"Yep."

"Have you ever hit a ball before?"

"A few times."

"Guess we can always use another...ah...fielder..."

"I'll be OK, I can take Right Field."

"OK."

Great, I'd done it: presented myself, shown I was willing to take part. Right in the middle of the vacant lot, with about sixteen other kids—waiting to be picked on a team.

Jeff leaned against a bat, which he used as a pointer selecting bodies. I waited, and waited, but I wasn't even picked. No, I was the very last person standing there; the odd ball, the no-choice, last chance leftover.

My own brother didn't even have the guts, or decency, to choose me instead of Johnny, who was only six and therefore pretty useless.

But I didn't mind—not really. At least I was doing something "constructive." And maybe after today, I was thinking, after I'd proved myself, I'd come out ahead of Johnny.

Robby Alfonsio was there too, for my very first game—picking his team. That's why I didn't mind being last. Last put me on Robby's team. And standing in line, watching Robby's eyes scan the possibilities only to pass—and rest—on mine, I *knew*. He had the eyes.

I saw and tried not to stare. But he definitely had the eyes and I kept checking, with quick glances, just to make sure. I couldn't believe it: there he was, living proof right there in my own neighborhood, going to school on my brother's bus, playing baseball in the vacant lot, and sleeping at night in a house within eyeshot of my own bedroom window. Wonderful. I didn't care if I made a fool of myself or not. Just turned and trotted across the diamond, heading in a complete dreamworld to my allocated corner of right field.

The living proof was his eyes—eyes that made my skin quiver and heart pound, inexplicably quickening the pulse and sending the imagination stark-raving wild. The very same deep-sea mirror that beckoned in my grandma's eyes, each time she showed me her ring.

So I knew from that moment on that Robby would transform my life, my outlook, my entire mind-set at that age, as I lived it on Oakhill Road. Without a doubt, nothing would ever be the same again.

I knew it because the next minute, with a reassuring smile, he handed me his own mitt. He gave me his mitt, and he used a spare. I thanked God to myself for that. In those few seconds my whole universe opened up and I was certain he was part of it. I carefully inched my fingers inside the leather, soft and damp from Robby's sweat and felt simply wonderful. I didn't care if I made a fool of myself or not. I turned and trotted across the diamond, heading in a complete dream world to my allocated corner of right field.

Chapter Four

The Knowing

Three weeks passed, and Becky waited—knowing. She knew it would happen, again, when the time was right. She had complete faith in the unspeakable thing. So she waited, and she was certain Clem waited too. Until sure enough, it was finally the day to deliver John's wedding shirt and she was once again heading toward Dawson's farm.

But all last week there'd been rain, and the mud was deep. Slow going, picking her way along the edges where the grass hugged the earth firm. Foot-sized ridges and cliffs gave way to her feet, slumped and gurgled as they disappeared into the mire.

Mustn't hurry, she was thinking. But no need to rush. The day was early, the shirt tightly wrapped and safe in her basket. A proper gentlemen's shirt, too, with the clean, fresh smell of new cloth, ironed, and white as snow. On the front, four perfect pleats followed each side, with flat pearl buttons, the generous sleeves draping down into wide, stiff cuffs.

Becky envied her sister's skill. But why so much fuss over a wedding shirt? John would wear it once, half hidden under a jacket and then it would be tucked away in a trunk. Saved for the occasional funeral.

To give it justice, she imagined the shirt on Clem and smiled to herself. Feet trudging through the mud, the early morning dew melting under the sun, the air still, the robins pulling fat worms from the ditches in the fields: she could picture the shirt, raw, on Clem.

He's running, chasing after her, along the row of poplars: white shirt unbuttoning, sleeves billowing, and arms flying—behind the shadows in the trees.

The grackles caw and flee. Flashes of white burst through the undergrowth. Leaves rustle, branches whip and dance, twigs crack. He's catching up.

He bounds out from the woods and blocks her path. Breathless. Shirt stained with sap and limp with sweat, cuffs rolled back, collar torn. The open folds of white cloth clinging to the heave of his chest, the curve of his throat, the turn of his elbows. Work hands hitched to his waist, boots splattered with leaves and mud, a strange smile on his lips.

"Becky…"

Her eyes wide, and silent. She can't speak.

He winces, as if in pain, and drops his hands. The crumpled pleats tremble, arms go limp.

"By God…"

Hands closing in a fist, fingers locking tight, he looks down at his feet. Shakes his head, boots pushing deeper and deeper into the mud.

Mutters, as if to the sinking boots, "I must have you."

Yes. And even when the spell broke, Becky stood motionless, transfixed. She fought the urge to fling herself down on the road, to wallow and kiss and laugh in the mud. Finish it.

She wanted to, but instead she forced herself to remember who she was. Remember her errand.

"It's a good 'un."

Old man Callum had just unwrapped the shirt and awkwardly fumbled as he tried to fold it back up again.

"Now you'll hang it up, won't you? If you don't it'll wrinkle," said Becky.

"Yep, yep." He put the package down and pulled a wad of kerchief from the pocket of his overalls.

"Thank yer sisters. Now go find Clem, he'll be loafin' by the barn. Should be loadin' yer eggs 'n milk in the wagon."

"Thank you, Mr. Callum. But…wait…you've already paid us too much."

"Naw, I'm givin' ya what's due. It's worth every penny. Now don't cross with me, you keep it."

Becky placed the rag filled with coins into the basket. She knew her sisters would be really pleased. Mr. Callum had been very generous.

"If my wife were still alive, she'd a heckled me to give ya more," Mr. Callum said, winking and then clearing his throat. "So's I'm jest doin' it fer her."

"Rest her soul."

"Yes well, she'd a wanted it. Till next week, then."

"Next week," echoed Becky. "We're all looking forward to the wedding and all."

And she stepped out the door, with the scruffy cats rushing past and heading straight for the hole in the siding under the porch, exactly as before.

But this time, walking up to the house, she hadn't seen Clem. When she'd passed the barn, he wasn't in sight. But she knew he wouldn't be far from the wagon.

"Clem? Are you there?" Becky wedged herself between the barn doors, cracked open, and stood near a stack of burlap sacks. The barn was dark, damp, and silent. But then she heard the whooshing crackle of dry straw, and the muffled clank of chains.

"Comin'…be right there," a voice murmured, from some unseen corner of the barn. It didn't sound like him. Not like Clem.

"I'll wait outside," Becky answered, feeling uneasy about what might (or might not) happen next.

Clem must have felt the same. For he brought out the wagon and hitched the horse without looking at Becky—not once. He seemed completely absorbed in his task, checking the wheels and fiddling with the reins and hopping on the wagon before remembering he'd forgotten to load the crate of eggs and milk.

He muttered something quick, had probably cursed, before he jumped off again to fetch the crate. Then he finally turned to face Becky.

"Ready, now. Hop on."

She blushed and held out her hand, but Clem's grip felt cold, and off-hand. How had it changed? she wondered. And why?

The wagon labored over the mud, the horse straining to make his load move. When they finally passed through the last Dawson gate, Becky attempted to speak. It was a struggle to sound normal.

"I'm not sorry, Clem. About what happened. You know. I mean, I hope you know."

"Good." His answer, given straight away.

"Doesn't it mean something? What happened?"

Clem must have noticed how Becky turned, facing him so that he'd return her gaze, but he kept his eyes on the horse.

"Well? Doesn't it mean something?"

"I'm not so sure."

Becky sighed. It was like an opaque mesh or curtain had been drawn, screening the possibility of carrying on. Clem's body, the air, the wagon, the road, all covered in a thick film of obstinate vagueness and distance. Not raw, not pure, and certainly not clear. Like scum.

But when they reached the same place in the road, Becky grabbed the reins and pulled the horse to a stop. She simply refused to believe it wouldn't ever happen again.

"Stop!" she commanded. "Clem, I want you to halt right now, right here, and look at me."

"Think about what yer doin'," Clem answered gruffly. His hands pressed against his forehead, eyes shut and jaw set tight. Body stiff with anger, or fear, or Becky knew not what.

"I don't need to think," she said, trembling now, and almost choking on her words. "For now I know why I was born—what I'm meant to feel."

"Then I'm thinkin' fer us both," Clem replied. His hands suddenly gripped her shoulders, hard. He stared straight into her eyes and Becky could feel the curtain slipping away.

"So ya want me? Gall darn, I got a heart, girl. But I ain't got no learnin'. What do I got? Alls I see is nothin', comin' ta no good. Got nothin' much ta give, Becky, that's why."

"Give yourself," she whispered. "Clem, I'd marry you, I would."

"So you would, then," he said. Eyes already swelling with emotion, hands caressing her neck.

For in that moment he let himself go, whirling and riding the swell of the mirror-sea, the waves of darkest desire reflected there, somewhere in Becky's eyes.

Then he believed, pulling her close and kissing lips with a feeling that lingered, long after the horse finally snorted and stamped, impatient to be getting home.

*

"You weren't bad—for a girl," Jeff admitted, after the game. We were home by then, eating supper.

I did manage to catch a high fly. But a low driver I missed, and I struck out at bat, twice. Come to think of it, I'd made other mistakes, along with a consistent display of lousy throws.

"I'll practice throwing, if that'll help," I said. "Maybe you can give me a few pointers."

Jeff nodded, his mouth full. But he'd never do it, of course. No matter, I was thinking. In fact, I wasn't that bothered about it. Even though I certainly didn't play well enough to impress Robby, I had no desire to improve my skills so he'd notice me—in return. Does that seem strange? Not for me, because that's not the kind of thing that attracts the nutbag. Even then, I sensed the difference: how being in love and scheming in the normal way is something else. A whole new ball of wax.

"Why aren't you good friends with Robby?" I asked, getting on to more important matters.

"Robby? He's in the school band. He's always practicing on his clarinet, or going to a clarinet lesson, or studying or something. He's definitely a loner. A bit odd, if you ask me. Don't get on with him much."

"Oh. But he's good—I mean I noticed what a good pitcher he is. Fast. Isn't he?"

"Yeah, he's as good as me. So far he's hit more homers than me—but you wait. We've got the rest of the summer yet."

I was dying to know more, but didn't dare ask.

And why? Why Robby? Those eyes burned in my head like a hot branding iron. It seemed inconceivable that I hadn't noticed them before.

The only thing I had noticed before was how Robby's clarinet case, like a ball and chain, set him apart in the line of boys and girls waiting at the bus stop each morning. The High School stop was at the opposite end of the road, so all I saw was the vague outline of his features; a lean, short body bent forward with a black oblong case dangling in front, sometimes the case bumping impatiently against his leg. Not the type you'd imagine to be any good at baseball.

But now, of course, I wanted to find out as much as I could. "Is he going to be a professional musician or something?"

"Can't you hear him practicing all the time?"

"That's Robby? I thought it was his mom."

I took another bite of my meat loaf and mulled it over. Of course everybody in the Alfonsio family played something. Robby's sister Vanessa played flute, his older brother Stephen played piano, his dad played violin and his mother seemed to dabble in everything. Both his parents were brains: PhD's and working for IBM, as research scientists. The music was just a hobby.

And the Alfonsio kids, seven in all, looked just like their twin-set parents. All had the smooth, olive-hued skin, greasy uncombed dirt-brown hair and bulbous, protruding lips. All short, skinny, and somewhat awkward-looking. Big round heads, long matchstick arms, stubby trunk bodies and short-shinned legs. Sort of the neighborhood's version of an Einstein clan. Only the Alfonsios weren't Jewish—they were Italian Catholics.

Robby wasn't an exception, though he was the only one in the family who didn't wear glasses. Not that glasses would have made any difference. I was careful to compare, and what I saw in his eyes set him apart from his brothers and sisters. It wasn't only intelligence. No, his eyes had something else too—*it*, the difference—and I wouldn't have missed that behind glasses, either. Of course I had no idea what *it* meant yet, but I was certainly going to try and find out.

"Do you think he'll show up for the game tomorrow?" I asked.

"How do I know?" was Jeff's answer, followed by a suspicious look. "Why are you so interested all of a sudden?"

"I was just wondering if I'd be able to use one of his mitts again," I said.

"There's plenty of those knocking around," Jeff replied. "Don't worry about it."

"OK." I backed off and finished my supper.

"Won't your father be pleased," my mother said, taking away my plate.

"It won't last," Jeff cut in. "She'll get fed up with it in no time."

But the strange thing was, I didn't get any satisfaction out of telling my dad, when he got home.

Somehow I already knew that not only was the baseball going to last, but for all the wrong reasons. As far as my dad was concerned.

CHAPTER FIVE

Robby

A good number of people had filled the pews. Becky and her sisters sat on the groom's side, passing smiles between friends and family before the ceremony began. St. John's church was a Catholic parish, so Mrs. Callum had refused to attend. Nevertheless she'd permitted her daughters to go, for any wedding in Philipsburg was an important social event.

Watching Rachel approach the altar, Becky felt her own pulse quicken, her own lips quiver. Soon would not she, too, be the center of attention? Yes, she was thinking, the bride looked nervous—but radiant. Rachel seemed to float on air as she passed, tucked securely under the arm of her proud father. She wore a simple white cotton frock, but artfully transformed—trimmed from top to bottom in layers of hand-sewn lace. Her veil, too, was fine lace embroidered in flowers.

Becky's sisters were certainly admiring the intricate patterns of the lace. This was painstaking work, creating cloth by needle and thread. Rachel's mother must have spent days and nights working on it. Now, sighs of envy mingled with the hushed, reverent whispers of other women as the bride moved past.

But Becky didn't envy Rachel's dress, her wedding, or her future. Like most young brides in Pennsylvania, hiding behind the flowers pressed against that virgin-white gown was a growing baby. What everybody knew (or guessed) slumbered within, had instigated—as usual—the rather hasty proceedings. A blossoming marriage, though not necessarily by choice.

Becky was thinking about this and her own state of affairs as she sat in the church. No, not pregnant, but she still felt sick. Nauseous. Almost dizzy, due to lack of circulation. It was unbearably hot and stuffy in the church. No cool relief from the stone seat in summer, or the sudden chill of a passing draft.

A heat wave in August. In Philipsburg. The month, the week, the day John and Rachel got married. The summer Becky began to see raw. The second, the instant, the unending moment of the year she would associate with Clem.

She could feel tiny drops of sweat trickle behind her ears and moisten the back of her neck under the plaited bun. She could feel Clem's presence in the church. Wherever his body sat, it was holding hers—and so tight she couldn't breathe.

Becky knew he must be sitting up front but she couldn't see where. She was sitting too far back and her sisters kept nudging and whispering. Interrupting the search. Distracting her.

"Such lace, Becky…Isn't it lovely…Doesn't she look happy, Becky…What's the priest saying…What does the incense mean…Oh Becky…Should we kneel…Will we sing…Are we to use the prayer book?"

Until Becky shook her head and said "Hush, hush! I don't know anything. You'd best ask a Catholic if you want to know more about their worship."

Then she realized how hard it was, just saying the word "Catholic." It stuck in her mouth like a piece of toffee, slipping past the tongue only to lodge stubbornly halfway down her throat. Unnatural and quite unpleasant.

Catholic. An obstruction. That gulping choke as she said it, and then a sick feeling: because she couldn't imagine how she'd ever tell her sisters, or her mother. She hadn't thought about it until now—how Clem was a Catholic—and for some reason her mother had a terrible grudge against Catholics. She wouldn't even set foot near a Catholic church. So Becky had this feeling "falling in love" was not a sufficient reason for wanting to marry one.

"Mother, I have something to tell you—I've made up my mind to marry Clem." As Rachel and Ben exchanged vows, Becky envisioned the scene. The shock and outrage of such a dreadful announcement, for that reason alone! A Catholic. Not to mention Clem was a farm boy, and uneducated. Had Mrs. Callum worked her fingers to the bone, sewing and mending all these years, so Becky could marry *him*? Not on her life!

"Don't expect any blessings from me," her mother would say. "No, just go ahead and break my heart."

How could she explain to her mother? Being pregnant was probably a lesser blow.

But Becky wasn't like most girls in the backwoods of Pennsylvania, and certain intimate pleasures of the flesh shared with a man...well...they just didn't make babies. Maybe she couldn't be sure, but Clem seemed to know. Those hands, those lips exploring the secrets of her body until the blood burned and the fire grew too hot to bear—how could she stop it now?

In church, defying the Bible. Not God. For every vein in Becky's body pumped with the news, and tingled in the knowledge: God is raw.

In the woods, with Clem, throwing away all words and thoughts. Letting the water, like magic, turn into the strongest wine; the body into the sweetest bread. Human lips touching the sacred Cup, blessed by the power of love.

In the world around her, pretending innocence, fearing ignorance, trusting freedom.

"Father, forgive me, for I have sinned…lusting after the flesh…."

She prayed for strength. Clem refused to go further, unless they were wed. Clem would never shame her. What more proof did she need?

"What God has joined together, let no man put asunder. Amen."

*

In summer, Maryland lies still under a blanket of haze: wrapped in a cover so thick and wide the glare of the sun is a blur, and the blue of the sky is somewhere beyond. Snuffed in a shroud of gray.

The stillness collects moisture. The blanket, all enfolding, increases the heat.

The air is heavy, like a dish of pea soup. Life is slow, sluggish.

Occasionally the leaves rustle. Just occasionally a fleeting breath of breeze touches the face, soothes the sweating brow. Only when the sun sets, and like the sun, passing gingerly—quietly—before sinking softly into the night.

During the day it's so hot nothing moves—except the unseen wings of crickets. The symphony of the crickets is continuous, unrelenting: the monotonous buzzing working to lull the brain, to deepen the urge to laze.

Shorn grass, mowed days ago but still moist, is the smell I remember. The smell of grass beginning to rot.

Not unpleasant, but part of the hot, still, bittersweet sense of summer. In Maryland.

On Oakhill Road the lawns are constantly being mowed. Piles of layered, matted grass sit in moldy, mountainous heaps rising from the ends of the lawns. Beyond the lawns runs a waist-high wall of thick, impenetrable growth.

Nature runs wild past the mowers, and no one interferes. The weeds—dense—grow taller and taller in the meadows, the nettles leaning and spilling over the verge. The stalks of corn in the fields—packed solid—are transgressing their allocated rows, and bursting fences. All of it, stem, leaf, bud, bloom, teeming with bugs.

In summer no one dares tramp through the woods. A jungle now, the trees covered in ribbons of creepers and vine; the undergrowth shoulder-high. Poison ivy charges through the paths, with pockets of prickclies, like landmines, couched in sorrel and fern.

Ticks hide in the grass, the brush, the woods, waiting for the passing of flesh.

But nobody moves.

Nobody moves until the oppressive heat of the day begins to wane. Then we emerge. The husbands pop their beers and start their mowers, the dogs bark and chase their rabbits, the toddlers circle the driveways on their tricycles, and the wives light the coals on their barbeques.

From five o'clock to six, we older kids loiter on the far end of the street with our radios. Count down the Top-Ten before dinner. Then, retreating back to our own separate backyards, we wolf down our Oscar Meyer hot dogs, or burgers with grease and ketchup dripping from the buns—and rush off again—just as the occasional breeze begins to ruffle the picnic tablecloth.

We've been waiting all day. The haze has lifted and it's finally time to play baseball.

I'm there. I'm always there, on Oakhill Road, pick any summer day, and I'm remembering—putting it in it's rightful place, the here and now. It might be a hot and humid afternoon, or maybe some evening out in the country, when I hear crickets. It doesn't take much. Maybe the feel of an occasional breeze, or the sight of an open field, dotted with weeds and trampled dust.

The part of me that's fourteen, it still lives. Especially that summer in Maryland. The day when I was standing on the vacant lot, praying for Robby to show.

Not that anyone would guess, as I was doing it silently. Praying, that is. While bending down to chalk the baselines. Lips moving, could have been mumbling anything. Like "shit, that was close!" after ducking a wayward practice throw.

In fact, it helped me keep my eyes off his house, but of course the minute his front door slammed I heard it. I was swapping bats and taking a few test swings, and bang my stomach went funny. Three Alfonsios come running toward us and one of them was Robby.

There'd been lots of games so far when Robby didn't show. But you could hear—from his house—the sound of his clarinet. Strains of chromatic scales and classic solos. He worked hard, practiced for hours.

I'm not sure what felt worse—having him there for the game or not. If he showed, he'd pick me to be on his team. I would try harder to play well, if only to disguise the real purpose of my being there at all. But when he wasn't around, and I should have cared less, I played just as if he *was* there. I tried even harder. I assumed he knew. Could see me.

I wondered why. Why was I so convinced he knew? That he had something for me, like proof? Nobody else had guessed—could possibly guess—what was going on between us. But I was certain. I knew Robby knew because he had the eyes. I watched how his eyes cut through the outward facade; how they caught the invisible thread. It was that, and nothing else, game after game, which kept me going.

Every fly I caught, every pitch where my bat made contact with the ball, every whoop of encouragement from Robby's team, was just a little reminder.

But that day I could feel in the pit of my stomach how tight the thread was beginning to tug. I threw down the bat and joined the rest, now a line-up forming in front of Robby and Jeff. Robby showed. Prayer answered and God, was I thankful.

A coin was being tossed for first up. Heads. Robby's team this time. The rest of us crowding the line in a sort of circle, anxious to start. My stomach still feeling really queasy.

No wonder. Robby in the flesh this time, and smiling: those deep, deep eyes squinting in a pleasing way as they surveyed the line. Right hand tucking in and out of the upturned leather mitt, thinking.

"Nina." No, he hadn't picked me yet, but I was already hearing him utter my name in the same tone of voice he used for the others, long down the line. No longer chosen last, but not too soon. Careful not to stand me out, or raise suspicions.

"Nina." He'd wait until it seemed like an afterthought, a sudden playful whim to be nice to a girl.

But I'd catch it. Only a flash, a brief second of a look followed by a knowing smile. He'd say Nina looking at me hard and thrusting that look for a second, straight into my eyes. That particular second would turn into hours of explanation—if you had to use words.

Enough for me.

But this time it never came. Head bent, left foot digging at the dirt, Robby announced his picks in a sudden fit of impatience. As if he'd rather be somewhere else. And much to my surprise, his eyes avoided mine, waiting and choosing others until Jeff closed in.

"Come on, Nina, let's go!" my brother shouted, as the teams were already taking position and I should have been well out there, in the middle of center field.

"OK, OK." But how could this be? I was in a state of shock, frozen to the spot in disbelief.

I wasn't on Robby's team. And not only that, I didn't have his mitt. Robby wasn't even offering. But didn't he always gave me his mitt, use his spare?

I suddenly had to decide what to do. Should I ask him for it? It just didn't seem right. I wasn't even on his team.

So I dashed to the pile of extra gear sitting in the ditch at the end of the lot—not looking at Robby or anyone—and scooped up a mitt, any mitt. Then I ran like mad to center field, and tried like hell to forget it, and simply play ball.

Forget it. With Jeff pitching, and Sammy at bat, and then Patty, and Deb, all hitting singles, all on base. I waited for Robby's turn, standing like a statue and staring like a zombie past the lot, and down the hill, to the valley in the distance. The valley now washed in mist and the orange glow of sunset.

Robby's turn. Something was up, and I wondered why the sunset worked; how it soothed the rough edges of the unfamiliar mitt, eased my troubled brow, promised that yes, all of this and more, had a reason.

For Robby seemed so different, that day. I, who noticed the every move, every inflection, every twist of muscle on that face, those arms, could see he was troubled by something.

He stepped up to the batter's position. Looked around. Took a deep breath, shook his head.

The fielders began to chant, the "yip yip" and chides rising in a high-pitched chorus, meant to distract him. I didn't move, the alien mitt lifeless and slumped at my side. Fingers itching to slip out and clench the open sky.

It was too much. The sweet balm of summer lingering in the air. The pinky orange sunset, in languorous brushes, sweeping out the haze. The smell of grass, mixed with honeysuckle and cow's lace. The distant rumble of a tractor plowing wheat. The subtle drift of pollen, circling gnats, curious bugs brushing bare arms. The stickiness of sap and human sweat. The feel of the ground under your feet, the endless green carpet of fields surrounding our hill.

Too much. All of it bursting and seeping—there and then—into every pore of my skin.

I could tell he was feeling it too, standing there the way he was standing there. Wishing against time, wanting more time. As if in slow motion, watching Robby move: bend down, squat, rise, tap the plate with his foot, chalk his hands, and finally twist the bat between both hands as if choking someone's throat.

"Come on, Robby."

"Throw one, Jeff!"

"Windup, Curve, yip yep!"

"Batter up!"

Then, before the bat was even poised, Jeff, growing nervous, threw his pitch. Robby didn't seem to care—his arms swung out like lightning and *crack*! the ball spun like a rocket. Clean out of sight.

After a moment of surprised silence there must have been yelling—but I wasn't paying attention. Instead I was staring straight at Robby who hadn't budged. Gripping the bat with both hands again, he looked as if he was actually staring straight across the field, right back at me.

"Nina! Nina! You got it!" now screaming from all sides, but I didn't hear my name, not then. When I finally looked away from Robby, it was too late. The ball, spotted by everyone else, headed straight up and out of sight, before dropping and finally landing—with a thud—right smack in front of my feet.

"Ahhhhh, jeeeezzzz..." the groans of disappointment burned in my ears as I stood, still rooted to the spot, amazed by it all.

I stared at the ball. It didn't move. Just sat in the grass smirking at my feet, like a dirty joke or a laughing gnome. Which made me instantly pull the mitt off and fling it to the ground. Then Johnny came running from left field, picked up the ball and threw it home—to no avail. I didn't even realize what Johnny was doing—only how Eddy Babcock finally grabbed the bat, and pushed Robby off, before Robby decided he better get himself to first base.

"What the heck's going on?" Jeff shouted. "Nina, what kind of idiot are you? To miss *that*? And how could you stand there like a dumb-bell, not even throw it back? Three runs! Jesus!"

"I don't know! I'm sorry," I shouted. "Besides, I've had it. I quit! Wouldn't have caught it anyway, not with this lousy mitt."

And without giving it another thought, I ran off the field, down the street, through the front door of our house straight to my bedroom.

What a big mistake. I kept repeating that to myself, over and over. Clenched teeth, eyes streaming. What a big mistake. Mistake, mistake, mistake. There wasn't anything in Robby's eyes. Nothing. Forget it. So what? A big mistake.

The tears were still wet on my cheeks when my mother knocked on my door. I had refused to come down and face the world. Especially my insensitive oaf of a brother, Jeff.

"Nina, you'll have to come out. Someone's here asking for you."

"At this hour?"

"Well, it's not that late, and it's Robby Alfonsio. He says he wants to talk to you."

"Talk to me?"

"That's what I said."

"Robby Alfonsio?"

"Yes, you heard me, Nina. Robby. I don't suppose he has anything to do with what's going on?"

No answer. I'm sure my mom was concerned, but she always preferred her kids to sort these things out on their own.

"Mom, I'm sure it's Jeff he wants to see."

"No, that's not what he said. Why don't you come down? He won't come in. He's standing outside the front door. Looks upset."

"Oh...all right..."

I was sure I was dreaming. I waited until the sound of my mother's footsteps reached the bottom of the stairs and headed into the kitchen. Then I crept down and found myself standing alone, next to the front door; and in the darkness, behind the screen, I could just make out the features of his face.

Robby.

That moment was so unexpected and wonderful that I vowed, there and then, never to doubt the nutbag again.

He was there all right, but put his arm against the screen to keep me from opening the door.

"Nina, listen. This won't take long. There's something you should know, and I want you to hear it from me."

Just like that, leaning his arm against the screen, voice shaky and excited, as if the words were being dragged out, dry and hollow, through the bars of a stone dungeon.

"I want you to know I picked you. Today, on my team. I know it looked like I didn't. I tried not to. But see, when you weren't on my team, well, you know. It made me feel awful."

I took a deep breath.

"No, don't say anything. I'm doing the talking and I want you to know I like you. I don't care what the others think. I like you. Not Deb, or Shelly, or Pam. They don't mean that much to me. So don't listen to what anybody else says."

This, with his arm so close, moving slightly, so as not to press so hard against the screen.

"I just wanted you to know how it is. With me."

Everything I said in return was gushing out in waves, sieving its way through the screen, and splashing over Robby's face. Using just my eyes.

In the brief silence that followed, Robby's look assured me I had never, ever, been mistaken.

"So...well...I've said what I came to say," he finally muttered. "And look, this is yours. I want you to have it."

And before I could say or not say another word, he dropped his mitt on the front doorstep. Turned away from the screen and marched like a real trooper across our front lawn. He never looked back, and gradually all I could see was his silhouette passing under the street-lamp.

Then the dogs down the street started to bark. I guess they could hear it too, a boy whistling in the dark, somewhere down the far end of Oakhill Road.

Chapter Six

The Fire

Quickly—in a flash—Becky had slipped through the crack in the barn door. Pressed herself against the splintered wood and listened closely for any sound of movement.

No sound. Just the cool, soothing silence of shade, empty stalls, suspended dust. The muffled coo of a dove. Her own breathing.

She looked up, high above the rafters, where the sun, in blinding slivers, was peeking through the roof. No sign of the spying dove, but something moved. Shuffled, like restless feathers. Then stopped.

"Clem?"

She whispered his name, wishing she hadn't come.

What if he didn't show? Or what if he did? They hadn't spoken. Not here, on the farm, during the reception. No, just gazed across the streaming ribbons and heads bobbing over banquet tables to acknowledge each other—in lust.

Her thoughts were in turmoil. Clem, she was thinking, please don't come…it's much too dangerous, meeting like this. The next minute: Yes, Yes, you must come, follow me now, to the—"

"Over here."

She turned abruptly, took one last look outside.

Through the crack in the door a crowd of people still clustered around the tables. The men already drunk from an unseen source; the women busy dishing out the pies and lapping up the gossip.

Clem waited in the shadows, half-hidden in a corner behind the milking stalls. She spotted him then, leaning forward to sling his Sunday jacket on a bucket peg. So he had understood, read it in her eyes. She smiled.

"Tell me how you knew," she whispered, reaching his side and feeling his hands clasp her neck.

"Quiet…I know nothin'…" he muttered, pressing her body up tight against his.

Becky leaned against the side of the stall. While Clem pressed his legs against her dress, he seemed to push her up and hold her there.

"…know jus' this," he said, suddenly slipping one of his arms from her waist, down, down and tight between her legs. Hand forcing a way in, past the skirt, slip, corset, panties—to reach it.

"Yes," Becky answered. And sighing, felt the ache start to melt, and drip, through his fingers.

He didn't move. The arm, the fingers motionless: instinctively, reaching deep to gently cradle her desire. Then, a feeling that seemed to lose all sense of man, woman, time and space—hand, inside her womb.

He said nothing more, holding her that way and moving from the stall so his own strength would take her weight. Holding fast to the sensation for so long, so very long, it seemed as if he'd never let it go.

And what if someone had seen?

A strange sight. No shame. A man. Standing in a barn.

Taking the flame like a pagan lighting a torch and lifting it—in awe—to the shadows.

*

"What did Robby want?" Jeff asked the next morning over breakfast.

Casual. No smirk, no funny smile. Just looked hungry, my brother. Popped a spoonful of Frosted Corn Flakes into his mouth and chewed.

I watched him. Crunching, slurping, not even looking at me—hardly what you'd expect from someone hanging in suspense to know the answer.

"Nothing much."

"Nothing much," Jeff repeated. Crunch, crunch. Swallow. "Didn't say much then?

"No." I watched Jeff swirl and clink his spoon, scrape that bowl down to the very last morsel. Then decided to add, "You wouldn't be interested."

"So you won't tell me."

"Tell you what?"

"What he said."

"Nothing much to tell."

"Then why'd he come over?"

"What do you care? He was just…being nice. Said I should stick with it. Baseball, and all that. To keep playing," I mumbled back. "That kind of stuff."

"Oh. But you couldn't tell me that."

"I just did."

"Yeah."

I watched Jeff shake his head, shove his bowl aside.

Wipe that drop of milk hanging from his chin—with his sleeve.

"Girls, who needs 'em," he snorted, rising off his chair. "I didn't think Robby. Jeez."

And before I could protest, he grabbed his cap and headed briskly out the door.

*

Becky and Clem married, in haste, less than a month later. Even an ambitious, intelligent woman like Becky didn't give it a second thought.

No, the moment Becky started to see raw and fell passionately in love with a man, she lost her common sense. She felt no shame in disappointing her mother. Completely transformed by the power of this new connection with Clem, she felt more alive than she had ever felt before. She had no fear or dread of what might lie ahead.

So they eloped. Ran off to Clearwater county and made the union legal. Came back, shocked Becky's mother, surprised her sisters, bemused the town. Helped, as numbers might help, rejuvenate the Dawson clan.

Now Becky had nothing but Clem and the farm. Her mother, arguably outraged, had disowned her. Any daughter who corrupts her soul, rejects her family, and turns to the enemy—is gone, dead. No longer any relation. Marry a Catholic? Not a Callum.

But there was a Mrs. Clem Dawson. A woman with a new pair of eyes, setting her hopes and dreams on something raw. A God-is-Raw religion. One ride beginning with the wagon and forever ending in the wood.

The scholarship was left behind. With no regrets, Becky made the most of her new role. She believed in it. Relied on her Clem's support to carry them through. And it did. At first. Life was rich and wonderful. Passion ruled. Everything else seemed rather stale and insignificant in comparison.

By the following summer their marriage had produced a son, named Andrew. A year later a second boy was born, named after Becky's father, Ben. Then Clem did something which (once again) surprised his family and sent the gossip running through town. He signed up to become a policeman.

Clem Dawson left the family farm in Philipsburg and moved his family further south, to Greenswood.

As it happened, the State Police were recruiting young men, so he applied. He was accepted. In September of 1928 Clem became a member of the Greenswood Police Force.

Becky packed up a few belongings and along with the babies, followed. Saying nothing more than just a hasty goodbye or two, and hardly looking back. Was she the one who instigated it all? Pushed Clem to make a move? If so, she never said.

True, Greenswood wasn't Philadelphia, but it was a step closer. The county was growing; new shops and homes were being built; employment was on the rise. The town itself sat in a big valley next to the Black River. The river was deep and wide, and a few factories still flourished along its banks. New schemes were under way to help the unemployed find work; to bolster the economy and encourage the underprivileged to better themselves.

Clem must have heard about these schemes. Read the posters wanting men to teach and train. For the State of Pennsylvania was in arms: bootleggers and whiskey stills running amuck, raking in the revenue, smuggling in droves through high roads of the mountains.

In Greenswood, Clem's boots were black, and polished. Smooth and clean, and knee-high. He wore a uniform, in navy blue—stiff collar poking his chin, shirt riddled with pockets and brass buttons—and a silver badge. Bound by black leather belt and a cross-strap holster.

He had a hat, Trooper style—a visor that tipped his nose and masked all expression.

In Greenswood Clem's horse was black, and chromed. No bridle, and deaf to coaxing—busy grinding oil and rattling bolts—a beast that coughed a bluish smoke. Ate gas. And smelled like burning rubber.

A different man, who gripped the bars of a motorcycle shipped from New York and funded by the Feds, to patrol the dusty roads of the Black River valley. Who lived with an educated wife and two sons, in a box-shaped house at Number Ten, Hazel Street.

And far from the worn-out fields surrounding the farm on the outskirts of Philipsburg, far away from the wagon and woods and raging streams of the central mountains…

Clem and Becky started to sleep in separate beds.

*

"Nina?"

"Yeah."

I had Robby all to myself. We were alone, in the woods, down by the old Mill. A relic from the past, our Mill—an eerie, deserted building. Sentinel to an abandoned rail.

"Do you ever worry about it?" Robby asked, "—about thinking too much?"

"All the time."

"Don't you think it's strange, how our thoughts are so alike?"

"No…not now."

"Should I stop thinking about thinking?

"Can you?"

"No."

"I didn't think so."

Robby smiled, and I did too. Yet we both felt nervous. It didn't make sense. We were just sitting there, talking. As usual.

I can't remember exactly how it started, but every Thursday afternoon Robby and I would meet at the bottom of the hill. Then we'd cross the main road and disappear down the narrow track running through the field. As the crop that summer was corn, we were camouflaged. So we trespassed. Squeezed through a gap in the barbed wire at the other end, and scrambled—on hands and knees—under a hollow passage in the blackberry hedge.

It was tough going, beating back the jungle to find the path leading to the stream. But once there, all we had to do was take off our shoes and wade our way to the old Mill.

But this afternoon, the fifth Thursday and last week of summer, we were faced with the inevitable reality that the here-and-forever-here was about to end.

"Well, it's back to school next week," I said, out of the blue. Right then, as if it might be easier, just skimming the surface. "I guess we won't see each other much. Both be busy with school, homework, and stuff."

Robby nodded. Wiped a trace of sweat from the side of his nose. Then lowered his hand to find a stone, imbedded in the narrow inch of ground between us.

I watched his arm. Took it all in, the smooth olive hue of his skin. The movement of his muscles making tiny circles with the stone. The grip of budding manhood, restless male fingers running grooves, rubbing up and down. The pressing veins, and crisscross lines etching out the moment. A pebble. Some handy dirt.

The usual hot and humid afternoon, the thin-boarded walls of the Mill (those that were left) held together by tendrils of honeysuckle and weeds. A ruin, the Mill, a place to go. A ghostly silence, and wild, and cool in the shade.

Our secret place. With Robby intent on his stone, I waited, and waited, for that arm to make a move and come to me. That arm. So close. I couldn't stop my eyes running all the way along: stone, hand, wrist, forearm, elbow, sleeve. The sleeve of his faded T-shirt loose, with a peek of armpit, sneak of hair, underneath. And a dark patch of sweat…

Suddenly I realized how strange it was, this new sensation of taking in every little detail of Robby's arm. I was mesmerized. And gazing down at his flesh, following every crease in the sleeve of his

T-shirt, I instantly remembered something. The wagon scene. Hadn't I felt this same feeling, when I'd first seen that vision of Becky and Clem on the wagon? Sitting in agony just as Becky sat, watching Clem's arms as they gripped the reins? Even the sweat…wanting to be part of his own sweat…

"Nina, I'm sorry."

Robby's voice broke in and the feeling vanished. The stone, in one quick thrust, was gone. Now just a splash in the creek.

"Sorry? About what?" I blushed, could feel my cheeks tingling and exposing my thoughts.

"I'm no good at this, am I?" he muttered. "For the last hour I've been wanting to kiss you, but I can't do it. I've never kissed a girl before."

"We're both shy, which doesn't help," I ventured, no idea what to do, what to say next.

"Thinking too much," Robby added, flinging another stone and then suddenly turning to face me.

"It's all right, really," I answered. "When the time's right, it will happen. You won't think about it. I mean, I'm not so sure I'm ready, either. If I were, you wouldn't feel so uncomfortable. Would you?"

On edge. Robby simply looked at me, and I knew what that look said. It said: Let's touch. Why can't we touch? Why do we think so much about touching that we can't bear to actually do it?

And I, with a dream-self bending over and pressing my lips inside the soft curve of his armpit: I couldn't do it, either. Not yet.

"True." Robby paused. "Better not…rush it."

"I'm not too young. Am I?"

Robby laughed, a soft laugh signaling relief—the awkward moment over.

"You're the oldest girl I've ever met," he said.

So we went back to simply sharing our thoughts, enthralled by the discovery that they matched, even better than a hand and glove, or ball and bat. You never know. Maybe even better than a kiss.

Because we never went back to the Mill. Guess I misjudged the nutbag, which is often a fickle thing: it's so easy to cheat and betray. But I didn't know that yet. I was young. Robby was shy. We were certain we'd have other days; certain there'd be plenty of time, plenty more chances.

In fact, only two days later, it all came tumbling down. The rain, the news, the scuzz.

I sensed something was up the minute my dad came home from work. He drove into the driveway like a demon, then screeched to a halt. Jumped out the car and couldn't get through the front door fast enough.

Right in the middle of a thunderstorm, but he didn't seem to mind the rain. Just stood in the kitchen, dripping wet, smiling, holding a big green bottle that looked rather suspicious, like expensive champagne.

Jeff, Teddy and I had just sat down at the table, expecting dinner. While our mother, without a word, decided to stick the roast back in the oven.

"We're moving, kids!"

"Moving?"

"Yep, to California!"

"*California*?"

"That's right."

"Why?"

"Why not? You'll love it there. Hollywood, Los Angeles, loads of beaches, sun and surf, you name it. Movie stars, fancy cars, high-tech schools, Disneyland…"

He trailed off, noticed we weren't looking very keen. Except Teddy. He'd caught the Disneyland bit.

"Wow, dad!" exclaimed Teddy.

"When?" I asked, glaring at my mom.

"Gee dad, you didn't even ask us," Jeff muttered, nicking tomatoes from the salad bowl.

"There wasn't time," my mom answered, grabbing his hand. "Now stop it."

"I know it's sudden," said my dad, "but the offer was smack dab on my desk this morning. I had to take it fast, before they changed their mind and put it up for grabs."

"Who?" Jeff asked.

"UCLA. The University of California, Los Angeles."

"When?" I posed again, this time louder.

"When? Well now, Nina. The plan is, you all will fly over with mom—next week—so you can start in your new school. I'll sort the rest, the movers, the house, then drive the car across."

Needless to say I didn't eat much. Hardly touched the roast while the rest of the family ate like wolves and giggled like hyenas. I was miserable, and they were all so excited.

Then, to top it all off, my dad took the bottle of champagne outside, to pop the cork.

"There's something on fire, out toward Germantown," he announced, coming back. "Probably struck by lightning. Looks like it might be the Mill."

And he was right.

The flames were so high, the smoke so thick, the glare so bright that the whole neighborhood showed up to watch it burn. Plus plenty of other people. Cars parked blocks away and a large crowd gathered round to gawk—reluctantly giving way to the firemen, the maneuvers of their trucks, and the spray of wayward hoses.

It must have been well past ten o'clock by then. In the midst of all the confusion, faces flickering in the darkness, fanning back the smoke, I looked for Robby.

But I couldn't find him. Ashes falling in my hair, choking with emotion, I started to panic.

"Robby!" I shouted.

Robby, Robby, maybe even half-screaming his name through the unending lines of people I rushed past...where, where? Where was he?

Too late. The Mill collapsed, with a horrendous groan and crackle—burst of sparks—that made me cringe. Shudder. Close my eyes. The crowd retreated further back, singed by the heat. Someone pushed, I opened my eyes. Stupid fool. I thought it was Robby, but no, just some kid, chasing another kid.

God, it was awful. Enough was enough. I turned away. Completely devastated, I headed back to the car.

And it hit me then, how Robby wasn't going to be around when I really needed him. Not now, not ever. All that remained was this dreadful feeling of how I'd always be alone, and all that was close to my heart would inevitably go up in smoke, the moment I felt bold enough to imagine I was holding some proof.

So I gave up. I stopped hoping. I mean, how could I expect Robby to find me in such a crowd? After all, he didn't know we were moving to California, and there wasn't much of a Mill to begin with. A typical thunderstorm. A heap of dry wood. A fire. Maybe the Alfonsios simply stayed home.

It was so unfair, I was thinking, to get this far only to have it all slip from my grasp and sink into a hopeless heap of ashes. No. I'd never get another chance to kiss Robby's lips, or relish that rare feeling I had with him, in the woods past the farm.

"Grandma, where are you? Please help me!" I suddenly moaned, fighting back the tears. "I need you...you're the only one who'll ever really love me..."

But of course as soon as I said it, Robby suddenly appeared. Right there. Standing a few feet away. His face, his tears, and all that was left of the Mill.

Had he been crying too? Or was it the smoke?

"Lets go," he said.

I shivered.

And like magic, stone fingers closed warm in my hand.

Chapter Seven

Clem

I never even asked my grandma how she got that ring. It wasn't her wedding ring. Her wedding ring was a plain silver band.

The questions she left behind I'm sure weren't meant to be answered—not in the sense of being spoken. That's the true test. If you've got the eyes, the unsaid always rings true. So we shared a secret pact: emotions so deep that words weren't part of the real connection.

No, she didn't have to explain, how a burning heart sits inside a ring. How it glimmers, and speaks. Tells me all I need to know: that she's going to die, but even so she'll still be watching; waiting for me to experience a glimmer too. Feeling joy when I get close.

The last time we did speak—using words—was over the phone, the day before the big move to California. She promised to come and visit. But a few months later my parents woke me up one morning in our new house in California to break the news. Then they flew to Pennsylvania for the funeral; left me and my brothers behind. She died, alone, one night in April, in her house of thirty-two years. The grandma who kept insisting "when I'm gone," had gone. Dead to the world, the wife of Clem and the woman the locals called Becky, the widow of Evergreen Acres.

My parents felt it was too expensive and depressing for us all to go. My brothers and I had never been to a funeral. Our Grandad died long before we were born. He had been killed in a strikebreaker's riot in Pittsburgh, in the 30's. Our mother was an orphan, so there weren't many relatives on her side to pass on.

I should have begged my parents to at least let me go with them, but I didn't. Even worse, I didn't show any sign of emotion. Strange, but the guilt over evading the sight of her lifeless body and the dirt that would cover her grave, made me feel dead. Cold. Distant. Unreal. Stone-faced, I simply said nothing. I could hardly believe she no longer existed. Bewildered and cheated of a real ending, I kept seeing my Grandma's loving smile and feeling the strength of her hug; the eyes that promised I'd always be special and precious.

Who would keep that feeling for me now?

When I'm gone, when I'm gone…and I kept wondering if I'd ever feel her gone. Perhaps I knew in my heart that as long as I didn't give in, or believe it, I'd be safe.

My dad was the one who decided to wake me up, by describing the final ritual. He said he felt compelled to lean over the coffin—at the Greenswood Funeral Home—and touch her corpse. He thought I should know, because something made him gently tap her shoulder and look down again—to her waist. His gaze moved from her powdered, unsmiling face to her arms, folded, and then to her hands. He studied her hands and suddenly remembered; slipped the ring off her finger, he said, like a thief, and hid it in his pocket.

He told me this a week later when we were sorting through a box of photographs. Of course he'd brought a few things (besides the ring) back with him.

I must admit my dad wasn't the only one who had forgotten about the ring, but the circle of blue sapphires had prevailed. Fingers splayed apart, my own hand trembling, I gazed in awe. It fit.

That's when I finally burst into choking sobs, and wailed like an abandoned child.

"Did Grandad give Grandma the ring?" I eventually managed to ask my dad, after drying my eyes on his shoulder. Suddenly it felt all right to be asking someone else.

"Yes, he must have," said my dad, stroking my head and making me feel so much better.

"You mean you don't know for sure?"

"No, but it must have been him."

"Why?"

"It couldn't have been anybody else. And she's always had it, as far as I can remember."

"But you said Grandma and Grandad eloped. They were really poor, lived on the farm, and didn't have any money."

"That's right. But then dad became a State Trooper. In Greenswood he started to make money. He got on well, and even became a little famous."

"Really?"

"Well, for one thing motorcycles were a real marvel back then, in the Thirties. And your grandad escorted the Governor of the State—once—from Philadelphia to Pittsburgh. That was a big deal, for people like him in those days."

My dad paused and fumbled through the pictures.

"Look, here it is. Here's a picture." He handed it to me.

I was amazed: this faded, gray-black image of a man in military uniform was my grandad. Posing proud on a motorcycle like a king sitting on his throne. Young Clem. He looked stern and formidable—more like a Marine than a civil policeman. His head tilted, chin out, eyes completely obscured by a dark shadow. But his mouth and lips were like my dad's. Soft and round, half-pouting, half-sunk in a stubborn scowl.

"But I thought he and Grandma didn't get on very well, I mean…they argued a lot, and you always said you didn't see much of him, as a child."

"That's right."

"And how old were you, when he died?"

"Only six. So of course I don't remember much."

"But you went to the funeral?"

"Yes, but that was several weeks later. Due to the circumstances, we had something more like a memorial ceremony. They never did recover his body."

"They never found his body?" I hadn't known that. Now why hadn't anyone mentioned it before?

"No." My dad was quick to add, "It happens, sometimes. A warehouse caught fire and a wall collapsed. Some remains were found, but many couldn't be identified."

"But I'm sure Grandma told me she went to Pittsburgh…"

"They showed her parts of his motorcycle."

"Oh." I was puzzled by this new revelation, but I wasn't sure why. "It must have been awful," was all I could mutter in reply.

"Yes, but—she carried on."

And my dad carried on too: continued to sort through the photos, most dating much later, when he and Ben were growing up into adolescents. This annoyed me. It was obvious I was touching an emotional chord, but my dad's stern expression meant he certainly wasn't going to reveal anything more.

"It just seems strange, Grandad giving Grandma this ring," I insisted.

But my dad wouldn't budge. He apparently had more pressing concerns. "Nina, listen," he replied. "You be careful with it. That's a real diamond, and those are real sapphires—must be worth a few thousand dollars if we had it appraised today. Whatever you do, don't take it off and leave it somewhere. I'm not so sure you should be wearing it."

"After all this?" I said.

But I wasn't really listening. I was staring at the picture. Seeing Clem on his motorcycle like that sent shivers down my spine. The image was so powerful that a scene was beginning to form inside my head: in the same spot at the back of my eyes where I saw the wagon.

God, yes, when I closed my eyes it finally happened again. I could see Becky. There she was, clear as day, crouched under a window. And peering through this window as she did, I could see a room full of smoke, and several men gathered round a pool table.

Clem was there in the room, looking just like his photo. But he wasn't wearing his hat, nor was he standing rigid like a stern Marine. No, he was laughing and waving a cigarette at an old man. While the rest of the group—all men—were passing money between them, and drinking.

My second clue. To how it all went wrong. For I could feel my heart sink like Becky's. I knew something bad was about to happen.

"Nina?"

"Yes?" I opened my eyes. My dad was shaking my arm.

"Haven't you been listening to me?"

"Sorry, no."

"I was saying we should take it to a jewelers for an appraisal. It's wise to have it insured."

"Ok, dad." I agreed. "And could I keep this photo of Grandad in his Trooper uniform?"

"Sure, if you like it that much."

I nodded, even though I didn't really like it. But this was the picture that triggered a second vision. After all these years, the curtain had finally opened again.

And behind that picture, taken in the autumn of 1930, I felt the disappointment; saw a disillusioned Becky. Invisible to Clem and these other men, but nevertheless determined to see for herself what was really going on.

*

By 1930 Clem hardly ever came straight home after his shift. His "duty" as a Trooper, he said, meant he had to do certain other things.

"Like what?" Becky had asked.

"Stop by Denton's, for a game of pool. Pass a few stories, have a few laughs with the boys," Clem answered. "There ain't no harm in that, is there?"

"No…"

But Becky had sensed Clem wasn't telling her the whole truth. Men were entitled to have their men's talk, and play pool, but there was something else, too. Something that was pushing Clem away from her.

For having a few laughs with "the boys" seemed to make Clem tense and irritable when he got home. He avoided Becky's eyes and even his touch betrayed an uneasy hesitation. He was holding back, and resented her sensing it. More often, Andrew and Ben were already tucked fast asleep in bed by the time he got home.

So finally in October, on another pretext, she asked her neighbor Mrs. Hartley to mind the children for an hour. At five past seven o'clock on a Wednesday she left the house; rushed straight over to the Grocer's, just six blocks down, and across the street from the Police Station.

She hid in the alley, and waited. Sure enough, at the end of his shift, Clem and a few other "boys" disappeared through the back entrance to Denton's Dry Goods Store. Denton's was just around the corner. So it was easy: Becky waited a few minutes, and followed. She listened from behind the back door, which was cracked open—tense and ready to scoot behind a handy woodshed if someone should approach.

Clem had already explained to her how Denton liked their company, and was glad to oblige. He had a pool table in the back storeroom, surrounded by boxes and extra junk, plus a few wooden chairs and a potbelly stove. The pool table was the mayor's. Years ago the mayor had ordered it as a present for his brother-in-law. Then they quarreled. So he changed his mind. Told Denton to "put the thing on hold." Clem obviously hoped Becky would find the story amusing: how Denton, after a while, forgot to remind the mayor that it was still there.

But Becky wasn't amused. She was suspicious, and didn't like it one bit. So much so that she was standing there now, spying from behind the back door. Straining hard to make out the conversation, through the rolling and smacking of pool balls.

"Hey Clem."

"Have a good day?"

"Humph."

"Catch any rum runners?"

"Nah…"

"Well git this…"

"Dibbs bets his last dollar—"

"That's somethin'…"

"Hopin' ta beat me."

"Nah…"

"But the darn fool does it again!"

"Nah…"

"Yep—he loses!"

Clem's unmistakable low-pitched laughter joined the others. Fitted in.

"Now that beats all, don't it?"

Becky could hear Dibbs laugh too, with his crazy chicken-like cackle. Everybody knew Dibbs: he was the town's most prominent bum. She wondered where the old fool got the money to place dollar bets. Dibbs, who always loitered along Main Street, with a big grin, black teeth, and tattered suit. Slurped his whiskey in broad daylight from a handy flask.

By the sounds of it, Dibb's "last dollar" never seemed to run out. And he certainly never went dry, either.

Becky grew bolder and crept to the window. She stooped, only raising her head high enough to catch a peek through the black grimy dust and glass of the lower windowpane.

She could see the pool table and several men. She spotted her husband, and gasped. Clem. With a cigarette in his hand, now moving up to his face, and smoke spurting from his lips. Clem smoked! The swirling cloud of evidence rose and merged into the thick blanket hanging over the green felt; the edges curling like snakes around the raised tips of cue sticks.

But that wasn't all: Clem's other hand held a square-shaped bottle, which was being passed around. The Troopers, Dibbs, and Mr. Denton—they were all filling small glass tumblers with it. Drinking whiskey!

Surprised as she was, Becky wasn't satisfied. This was small-time stuff. No, there must be something else. It would take something far worse than smoking or drinking moonshine to bother the conscience of Clem.

Of course she should have suspected playing pool at Denton's included a shot or two of whiskey. Clem never smelled of liquor, or tobacco—but he kept his distance. Probably rinsed his mouth with baking soda before he walked in the door. In that respect Greenswood was no different from the backwoods of home. Whiskey, rum, beer—all made, sold and drunk behind the women's and revenue's backs.

Besides, Clem's unit wasn't after people like Dibbs, Becky was thinking—who sold a gallon a day for his dollar. Nor a man like Denton, who probably had a barrel stashed under the floor. No, they were after the big-time; the truckloads of crates and tanks carried by gun-slinging thugs, and syndicates. They wanted the rich, who kept getting richer; or the agents, who after a few bucks gave the bootleggers their blessings.

So. That's what Becky was thinking as she moved away from the window, closer to the open back door—where she could hear.

"Did ya git some sense outa that youngster ya caught yesterday?"

"He perked up..." (Clem's voice) "a bit, after I offered ta give 'em a ride on my machine. But he had ta fess first, who he was runnin' fer."

"And did he come round, and fess?"

"Nope. Smart 'n tough, these kids. Seven years old, and he says, `why should I fess, jes ta ride behind yer ass, like a girl?'"

(Dibbs chuckling) "He's usin' his scrawny legs right now, but jes you wait. He'll be haulin' it under our nose—by the case, drivin' a Ford...before too long."

"Yep."

Which made Becky wince. For back at the farm, Clem's own nephews could easily end up doing the same thing.

Then, without warning, she heard footsteps coming her way. Leaping across the weeds, she managed to hide just in time.

It was Denton. He went straight to the woodshed. Opened the lock on the door, which swayed open with a groan, and disappeared inside. A few minutes later he came out again, bent double and huffing. Becky caught a glimpse of him staggering back inside with a heavy wooden box.

Unnerved by the close call, she decided it was time to leave. Quickly—hardly daring to breathe—she crept out from behind the shed. Passed in front of the rickety shed door. It was still open. She glanced in.

Her heart sank. Before her, in the darkness, she spotted the crates, piled in slumping towers and illuminated in the moonlight. The evening glow just bright enough to read what was stamped, in white, on each and every box: "Fleischmann Whiskey. Ohio's Finest Distillery."

The big-time. Right there in Denton's shed.

*

We wrote. For about a year, maybe a bit longer.

But I could tell by the letters that Robby and I were drifting apart. He'd send me pages and pages in a frantic scrawl, explaining how and why he'd become a born-again Christian. I wasn't surprised, knowing he was as spiritual-minded as me, but eventually I started to resent it. His letters turned preachy. He insisted God wanted those who loved Him to abstain from sex until marriage. He was rather upset when I didn't agree.

Meanwhile, I was still searching to find my own answers. Out West. And nowhere near the Bible.

It wasn't hard adjusting. Not in California, where everything seemed to sparkle in the sun; breathe deep and vivid under a clear blue sky. The San Fernando Valley was crowded, but who noticed? Pretty hard to complain, surrounded by palms and perpetual bloom; balmy beaches and sherbet sunsets.

I suppose looking back on it, I was pretty sure Robby was mistaken. After all, the nutbag seemed to me to be about as close to God as you could get. And the nutbag was divinely physical, too. So what was wrong with wanting to feel really alive—well before marriage?

So in High School I started dating boys who didn't have the eyes, but who did attract me—physically. Of course I couldn't help but notice the difference. For one thing, you've got to be careful when the fire starts in your blood. The body can be a real trickster.

I know because things started to happen again, with Kurt Grender. My senior year, I noticed Kurt sitting in the front row of my American History class. I noticed—like any girl would notice—how he was tall, blond, bold, and smart. Kurt Grender. The one always raising his hand and asking impertinent questions, or giving clever answers. His smile broad; his teeth perfectly even; his attitude blatantly conceited.

At first I wasn't impressed. Not at first. But I kept staring at him—or rather the back of his head—during class, like I was impressed. Or jealous. I don't know. I'm not sure why. But anyway, he must have sensed it.

Because in California, I'd taken up tennis. My best friend Paula and I liked to practice after school. We'd play a few games on the school courts before heading home. And that's when Kurt approached me: out of the blue, one afternoon on the tennis courts.

I was serving, and suddenly spotted him watching us from behind the fence.

Double fault.

"Love, fifteen" from Paula.

Fault again, then a slow, over-cautious serve that Paula whacked back so I hard I didn't even attempt to try and reach it.

I couldn't concentrate. Kurt's standing there, alone, was like an omen. He was smiling, foot-baller arms folded across his broad chest, blond hair falling in fine tousled strands over his forehead, long legs in jeans and straddled firmly apart like a Trojan on guard. Watching our every move through the chain-link fence.

"Love, forty."

I was angry that his presence affected me. That he knew it, too. So I took my last serve by tossing the ball real high—and swinging my racket down on it with all my might.

"Nina!" Paula shrugged. "That was stupid."

"I know." But I didn't care. At least the game was over.

Still, Kurt didn't move. As we were collecting our balls he moved even closer to the fence. I tried not to stare, but noticed his hands grip the chain-link fence.

He was hanging on. His fingers, like flexed talons, twisted around the steel mesh: positioned for my approach.

He simply locked his hands in the fence the minute I started to walk over. A signal I would have to confront him now, with the last fluorescent-lime Spalding lying just inches away from his feet. My eyes bounced past his mouthwash grin, his flexing arms, his hairy legs, his baggy white socks, his scuffed black trainers: a hot-headed, blurred chain of images, in that order, as I bent down to retrieve the ball.

He spoke first.

"You're in my History class, aren't you?"

"Yes."

"I'm Kurt."

"I know."

"And you are...?"

"Nina."

"The one who never talks and always sits in the last row."

"So?"

"I take it you don't like people watching you."

"No."

I was sure he didn't really care what I said. Our conversation was merely an excuse to keep it up—this physical assessing. He was blatant about staring at my body, like some boys do, and I realized he probably would have never noticed me. Except for my tennis-bouncing breasts and exposed upper thighs.

"You need more control over your serve."

"No kidding."

"I could show you how I do it, sometime."

"Sure."

"I mean it. What about tomorrow?"

"All right, then."

All right? Was I out of my mind! Yes. But the more I looked into Kurt Grender's sky-blue eyes, the more I wondered if there might not, after all, be some trace of a nutbag there.

So the next day he showed me how to improve my serve. Pointing my racket just so, raising the height of my toss, keeping my eyes off the opposite court. We rehearsed the motions, worked up a sweat.

It seemed so amazing, how little it took, to bring us together. We'd just met, and two hours later he was kissing and feeling me up behind the locker-room building. I'd never been kissed like that before, with experienced lips and tongue insisting—persisting—until the warm, melting sensation completely obliterated anything else.

The unhooking of my bra, the hands squeezing the swell of my breasts and cupping my nipples: I wasn't aware of how, or when exactly, he got there. Or whether or not we might be seen: me, half-dressed and legs apart to accommodate an exploring hand; he, moaning and writhing with a hard-on about to explode.

Only then did I understand why I had been drawn to him, right from the beginning.

*

"Clem, we need to talk."

Becky had put the boys to bed. Outside, the first snow was beginning to fall. She reached for her shawl and wrapped it around her shoulders before sitting next to him. Slumped in the corner of the sofa, Clem didn't respond. He was either half-asleep or staring vacantly into the fire.

"Clem."

"What?"

"Talk. Tell me what's the matter."

"Nothin'."

"There is. Something's wrong."

"You think so, eh?"

"I know so."

"Like what?"

"You're not happy."

"Then make me happy."

"I could if you'd help me. Talk to me."

Clem shook his head. "Want me to tell ya? I'll tell ya," he muttered. "Stop pesterin' me all the time, pickin' my brain about things that don't mean nothin' to me. I can't talk about what I'm doin'. I'd be happy fer some peace. Not pesterin'!"

"Oh I see," Becky answered. Not a good start, but she was determined to go on.

"I still love you," she said. "Do you still love me?"

"That's a fool thing ta ask," he grumbled.

"Why?"

"You're my wife!"

"You don't have to still love me, though."

"That ain't it," Clem answered, throwing a look at Becky that left no room for doubt.

"It's work, then? Something to do with work?"

"Becky, there's nothin' to tell ya."

"I wish we never left the farm."

"No ya don't."

"I do now."

No reply.

Of course that wasn't exactly true. And Clem knew it. She did miss the farm, in some ways. But she didn't really feel at ease there. The caring for the animals, the daily chores, the crops of vegetables and hay, the hard labor, none of it quite enough to disguise a growing sense of her own futile efforts to fit in. Rachel was much better equipped at resigning herself to the ways of illiterate men and the backward mentality of the farm. Becky was worried, too, about raising her children alongside Rachel's and Ben's. Would her boys skip school like the Dawsons, or choose to be more educated, like Becky?

"All right, I don't really want to go back," she said. "Greenswood has its advantages. The boys will get a better education. We're eating good, and you're respected. I've got time for my books, and a library just down the road." Becky tried to keep her voice steady. "But Clem, you were different at the farm."

"No I wasn't!"

"Yes you were!"

"How's that?"

"Well…back home you were…honest."

"Bite yer tongue, woman," Clem snapped, "If yer thinkin' to accuse me of lyin'!"

"No Clem, not that. But I've got to say, I know you smoke. You've been hiding it from me. That's not being honest, is it? Please, don't hide things from me. That's what I do mind."

"You seen me at Denton's?"

Becky nodded.

"When?"

"It doesn't matter."

"Gal darn, Becky, it does. My wife spyin' on me?" The thought seemed to jolt Clem upright like a man strapped to an electric chair. Rigid with anger, he finally glared at her, long and hard, eye to eye.

"You don't trust me?" he exclaimed. "Me, who's lain with you like I have? Then to be snoopin' on me, like I'm not bein' true to ya? My God, you should know me, Becky, to the core. That's enough."

"No," Becky insisted. "That's not enough. If being a Trooper makes you think like that, for God's sake think again."

"You don't want me bein' a Trooper, then? Changed yer mind, eh? After all I done to please you, Becky, 'n get us here?"

Becky listened stone-faced, wrapped rigid in her shawl. Maybe she wanted to fling herself at Clem's feet, and bury her head in his lap. But she couldn't. The raw power of love had slipped away, like flour through her kneading fingers. It had all gone to powder. Left her and Clem to fend against the scuzz like this: bitter and defensive.

"You like being a Trooper, don't you?" Becky asked. It wasn't a question, though.

"Yep. Darn right, I do."

"Do you think it's the best thing that's ever happened to you?"

"Nope."

"Then what's the best thing?"

Clem's jaw tightened. His anger struggled to keep silent.

Becky waited. Would he say it?

"Us, 'n the woods."

Yes! Becky bit her lip. Thank God, her Clem was still alive, somewhere inside that outer shell.

"What's happened then? To us in the woods?"

"We came out. Didn't we."

"I still hope..." she insisted, "to get it back, here—what we had in the woods." Even the distant memory of those bygone days was enough to make her catch her breath. There had been a time when she lived on those moist pouting lips, and yearned for the touch of those nearby hands. Might she not still feel that way now?

Clem leaned forward and stared into the fire. He studied the burning coals long and hard, before turning to face Becky.

"A man's pride can't be caught," he said. "Not by hook, by net, nor clawing sneaky like a cat. You don't trust me, now do you? Not fishin' like ya are. I can't abide my woman not trustin'...thinkin' she always knows more!"

"You want me to say nothing?"

"We did fine, like that."

"No," Becky exclaimed. "No, you're wrong. We just have to try harder. Find a new way, past the woods."

"Your way," Clem mumbled.

"Yes! Talking!"

But Clem wasn't ready to comply. He glared back at her and shouted: "To hell with it, then!"

"So that's how you want it!"

"Darn right!"

And he stomped out. She heard him put on his coat and slam the front door. She let him go. Straight to the station.

Let him sleep there, she was thinking. That night, so disappointed and disgusted herself, she vowed not to sleep or speak with Clem again until he admitted he was wrong.

A vow. A stubborn silence and separate beds, for a week or two. In Becky's mind, a pretty fair price to pay.

A test. For if Clem truly loved her, even now—he'd talk. Yes, he'd tell her everything. Pour out his heart and admit what was going on; own up to this big-time business. And then, no matter what happened, she'd back him up.

CHAPTER EIGHT

The Scuzz

After Kurt, I completely lost track of the nutbag. So there isn't much evidence, when you think about it. I wish there was just a little bit more.

Which gets me to where I am now, at UCLA pretending I'm an economics major and remembering past incidents to prove there were times when I did feel it. Though right now, the signs are so scarce I'm beginning to panic. Lose heart. Wonder if I'm stark raving mad. Back to the laughs and sniggers, "What are you on?" The seat of your chair? LSD? Mushrooms? It takes drugs to have visions…

But I'll say it again: apart from the nutbag, most of my life is bullshit. Sick, greedy, self-serving, defensive and predictable bullshit. But wait. Haven't you ever had a moment when you see differently and catch it, like the sparkle of Becky's ring, and you're a flame, aflame, a glowing star? A beacon of the universe? And don't you ever wonder what makes it happen?

I do.

So I'm sitting here in my college apartment with a pile of books on the table meant to distract me: but I keep seeing the freckled boy. Thinking about those eyes and those freckles with an Economics 3A notebook open to today's lecture, full of blanks where there should be graphs full of share curves, a list of falling interest rates, and a few loopholes for tax shelters.

I should be reading, writing, studying. Learning how to make money. That's what I should be doing. Not this. Not filling in the blanks of my grandmother's past, or trying to explain a nutbag and a sapphire ring. Or a freckled boy's sadness.

Still. I take up my reference book, *America: A Financial History* until I find the section covering the 1929 Stock Market Crash, the focus of today's lecture. The Crash. Rather appropriate chapter, I'm thinking. 'There's signs it could happen again.' Signs: but don't I know that already? Everything always comes crashing down.

I'll bet the freckled boy made the mistake of asking if people today would jump out of skyscraper windows—in this Age of New Technology. There's therapy these days for those who've been fucked; home computers, sleeping pills, secret cults, talk shows, psychoanalysis, credit cards, loan sharks and who needs money. Maybe that's why some of the students laughed.

It seems a shame I didn't catch him afterwards, because I could have asked to borrow his notes. A good excuse. Why, he might even be sitting here with me now.

I nibble on my pen and wonder what he's like in bed.

Naked, and…skin so fair it turns beet red when he's…embarrassed…I imagine his embrace and see flailing elbows, knocking bones, an exigent pressing like a flat knife against chicken's ribcage; frizzy hair bouncing like a runaway sponge. And I wonder, where do the freckles stop?

Anything's possible. I'm pretty sure I'm right. Even from a distance, his gaze so acute it smacked my forehead like a smoking fireball, and sent me reeling. Yes, the freckled boy would understand the whole story. Every last nut in the nutbag. I wouldn't have to leave out a thing. Not even Kurt. I mean, wouldn't he be glad to hear how a jock like Kurt knocks up a virgin?

Because in the San Fernando Valley, there's no hedge, no woods, no Mill. No place to go but up and down the four-lane boulevards, making eye contact at intervals dictated by the traffic lights, until you end up at a fountain in the middle of a shopping mall. Smoking cigarettes and sitting beside other cohorts like a ring of monkeys in a circus, shrugging shoulders and looking cool.

Everything moves. Cars, signs, shopping trolleys, skateboards, wheelchairs, plastic bags and credit cards.

Babies scream and mothers moan. There's *Raindrops Keep Fallin' on Your Head*, on and on. And on. Or a soothing Manalow drone. Exotic orchids and waxed rubber trees sway in the air-conditioned waft of candy and perfume. Polished floors muffle the squeak of sneakers and slip past heels. Manikin women and designer men loiter the racks, tempted.

But I decide. Craving to hold and to have the goods, I move, motion, promise, entice the inevitable on. And why not Kurt? Blue-eyed blond right tackle, number six pick for the Senior Prom. He's roused my passion, and he'd like me to go all the way. And so I will. He's that smooth.

I'm seventeen and wanting the next nut so bad it can't not happen.

The day before Kurt and I were slumped in the back seat of his car, wrestling with our clothes. Legs and arms squashed in the crevice where the seat belt hides under the cushion.

Right in the middle of this half-panting, wet lip-locked struggle, I pulled myself up and grabbed Kurt's hand. Just when it was about to thrust his keen and rigid rod past the soft nylon of my panties—into gear.

"Nina, what's wrong?"

"I'm sorry, but I'm not very comfortable."

"Am I squashing your arm?"

"Yes, and…I don't know…I've never done this before."

"Oh." His blue eyes softened for an instant. Hormones thwarted by a slight setback of surprise.

"Don't stop…I mean…I really want to."

"Don't worry," he said, hands gently flexing down my back. "We'll take it slow."

But I stiffened. "It just seems like it might be better…easier…somewhere else."

"Like where?"

"I don't know!"

I assumed the nutbag disappeared because I really didn't want to do it in the back seat of his black Mustang.

But Kurt couldn't think of another place to go. There weren't any woods or private plots of park in the Valley. So we drove up and down the boulevards. Ended up at the mall. Sat by the fountain and sulked. Then some of Kurt's "cohorts" arrived, and joined us. Eyed me like I'd already done it.

I didn't let myself consider the possibility. Would Kurt brag about certain intimacies with a girl like a quarterback who scores? No…surely not…but I sat there like his trophy. Solemn, mute and frozen in a fleeting sense of self-glory.

Finally, the "cohorts" left for football practice and Kurt, at least, felt better. He'd cracked some really good jokes and the mall-crowd had lightened his mood.

I decided to try again.

"Kurt…?"

"Can I help you?" he answered, with a Macy's smile.

I almost said something else, but changed my mind.

"Yes, I'm hungry," I mumbled. "Do you have any Jumbo Red Licorice?"

"I'm afraid not," he chirped, still playing the syrupy-sweet sales clerk. "But we do have a nice selection of chocolate covered balls. Care to sample some?"

"OK."

"I'm sure you'll find them much more satisfying than Licorice. And besides, they're on offer."

"Now?"

Kurt leaned over and ran his fingers through the trickling splash of a fountain.

"Tomorrow," he said.

"Tomorrow?"

The Macy's voice broke off, and Kurt's next play was put forward in a huddled whisper: "My mom's out all day. Fake a pass, meet me ten yards down the hall and we'll have the whole house to ourselves."

The next day I was opening the door to his black Mustang and without a word, letting him drive me to his house. We should have been in school but instead Kurt was teaching me something much more fundamental.

Or was he?

The feeling was wrong, this pre-packaged box of second-choice chocolate balls.

So I didn't let it happen like that, did I? My first time, with a guy like Kurt—in his parent's bedroom in broad daylight?

I guess I hoped the feeling would change.

And Kurt had already unzipped his jeans.

"Wait…do you think we should be doing this here?"

"Better than my bed," Kurt muttered, throwing back the plush velvet bedspread and catching me off-guard. Arms reaching out and wrapping me tight; my own cover dropping on thick shag carpet. "Now stop worrying, would you?"

It seemed to me then that whatever had drawn me to him had abruptly slithered away. Every sensuous move felt like a calculated pass, a mechanical means of reaching the goal. No doubt about it, Kurt had a gorgeous body. But running my fingers through his blond hair and feeling the firm muscles in his thighs move my body into place, I wasn't fooled.

It wasn't enough.

I tried to remember how I felt with Robby.

But Kurt's eyes were like steel marbles, glazed and shiny. And smooth, smooth, rolling on solid ice, blindly suspended, then falling, falling, faster and faster on sheer momentum.

All slick surface. No depth.

There wasn't a chance in hell I'd feel any passion.

He managed it, though. With a sudden giving up on me and coming quickly, before we both changed our minds.

True. It still makes me feel sick, whenever I think about it. Even now: but the freckled boy would be grateful. He'd listen and start to believe in himself. His eyes would shine, like a living Jesus—forgiving me all my sins. Unclean as I am, lusting and having sex with a dozen Kurts before I learned my lesson.

And then, what awkwardness between us? None. No, for his own fire—unrivaled—would flare, burn, and melt the barriers of freckles and scuzz.

*

Becky went shopping every Tuesday. She took six-year-old Andrew in one hand, and toddler Ben in the other, and headed for Lincoln Street. Andrew dragged the shopping basket along, until they reached the corner of Bishop and Lincoln.

Andrew was dropped off first, at the brick schoolhouse rounding the corner. Andrew—her Andrew—was already going to school. But he seemed to like it just fine, and why shouldn't Becky feel proud? Andrew

Dawson was a happy, confident and affectionate little boy. He could already read. And write. His doting, ambitious mother had been teaching him (before he could even talk) at home.

So Andrew handed the basket over to Becky when they reached the corner, and he trotted away to school. His brother Ben—feeling left out—would cry, but Becky always promised a sugar cookie from the Baker's. This usually soothed the wails into a whimpering sniffle.

Thus Becky was a prudent shopper, restricting her own appetite and attire in ways that might afford a few luxuries for her children. Clem said she spoiled them rotten—but she knew he was inwardly pleased. These days, if Clem said anything, it meant he was watching, and caring. Affected by what she did.

For the vow and battle of silence was still in operation, three years on. Becky and Clem, a wife and husband "at odds," spoke to each other only on rare occasions. They communicated in hints and half-phased fragments, through the demands of daily routine or the needs of the children.

"You'll spoil 'em rotten," followed by a gruff guffaw and a slight curl of a smile (instantly switched to an ineffective smirk) was something more. The Tuesday after, Becky was still thinking about it, as she walked down Lincoln Street with Ben.

Clem had been watching while they sat at the kitchen table, drawing cows and cats. The morning's surprise had been a colorful array of new pencils and crayons. Becky liked to begin each day with a different surprise.

Of course he didn't join in, or watch for long. But Clem spoke. Not your typical "I'm going out" or "can you wash my shirt" or "pass the gravy." No, this was sharing a feeling! In fact, Becky had smiled when he said it. He too, must have realized she'd caught him slipping.

The physical standoff had been achieved by her commenting, some time ago, that "the bed was too soft," and "you're starting to snore." No further discussion required and enough, as it were, to send Denton's delivery truck to their front door, with a pair of new mattresses to fit two single frames. At night, Clem would climb the stairs to his separate bed either well before or after she was ready to retire.

So aside from the occasional slip here and there, Becky and Clem managed to live apart, together with the children. Life carried on: Clem as a Trooper and home provider, Becky as a mother devoting her life to her two sons. In between, Clem went to Denton's and God knows where; Becky went shopping on Tuesdays.

Her first stop was always the Baker's.

"Hello, Mrs. Dawson."

"Good day, Mr. Godfrey."

"A sugar cookie and two loaves of rye bread?"

"Yes, thank you."

Then down the street to the Grocer's, where Ben (still chewing the cookie) stood quietly by her side as she checked for ripe tomatoes or weighed the beans. Ben knew it wouldn't be long before his mother's soft, coaxing voice would summon up his favorite count…"one, two, yes that's it! three, four…" as she tossed objects into the basket—plump purple plums or large green apples. Sometimes, if he got it right to ten, she'd let him choose a whole bag of penny candy.

On good weather days, coming out the Grocer's, Becky and Ben would saunter past the other shops. She'd stop to look at what might catch her eye, or simply daydream through the windows.

This Tuesday, in the middle of May, the second-hand shop displayed a tempting array of leather-bound books, crystal and jewelry. Becky stopped for a closer look.

The books were in good condition, the titles of Shakespeare and Milton in letters of gold; the crystal glasses with intricate grooves and shapes; the jewelry spilling out in splendor from a mahogany case.

And inside this case Becky saw a ring, nestled between an ivory brooch and four silver hatpins. She studied this ring; counted eight blue teardrop sapphires set round a single diamond. For a moment, she imagined herself on the other side of the glass window…

"Mommy?"

"Wait, darling," Becky answered. "If we had a study, Ben—" she suddenly exclaimed, "Oh how I'd fill it with hundreds of books! I could be Jane Eyre, and Clem—Rochester—and we'd be free of this curse. I'd wear silk and sapphires…"

"Sapphires? Did ya say Sapphires?"

Becky turned to discover someone had been standing—or hiding—in the doorway of the shop.

As soon as he stepped out and faced her, she realized who it was: the drunkard beggar, Dibbs.

She blushed.

"Oh excuse me, I was talking to my son."

"A good boy, too, eh…he listens, I kin tell."

Becky was about to walk away, but Dibbs pointed a shrunken finger close to her nose and insisted, "A sapphire, yes, is a mighty precious stone, strong 'n lovely, 'n powerful too, like yerself."

"Do you want some change? Here, take it."

Dibbs winked and smiled, but his eyes said no. Becky clenched the two nickels in her fist, keeping them hidden against the lower folds of her skirt. Ben pulled at her other hand and she wondered what to do next.

But Dibbs wasn't finished.

"…And the tent shook, fer mighty Saul shuddered—'n sparkles 'gan dart, from the jewels that woke in his turban, at once, with a start…all its lordly male sapphires, 'n rubies courageous et heart."

A beggar, quoting a poem by Browning? Becky knew it well, and the shocking recognition held her rooted to the spot.

"Male sapphires…" she repeated.

"As opposed ta female, bein' sky-blue, like yer ring in the window," Dibbs added, with a crooked grin.

"It's not *my* ring," Becky replied.

"Yes, 'mam, excuse me—but I sees it," Dibbs drawled, hiking up his trousers which kept slipping down his gaunt, bony frame. "If woke, tis yours!"

Becky frowned, but said nothing to dissuade him further. For Dibbs was right, she'd spotted the sapphire ring—which triggered the fantasy. And Dibbs—he knew. It made her tremble, and the way he looked at her. Strange.

The whites of his eyes were bloodshot, but the large black pupils held a glint—like a distant flash—of a long-lost dream. A wisdom. A knowing: disguised in filth and drowned by dark despair. Buried somewhere.

"Do I know ya?" he asked.

"No," Becky replied, still trying not to stare.

"I dunno, ya remind me of someone," he muttered. "Greenswood yer home town?"

"No, it isn't. As a matter of fact, I'm from Philipsburg."

"Nah, can't be!"

Dibbs suddenly shuddered and reached for his flask. He gulped down the liquid, smacking his lips and screwing the cap back on, all the while completely ignoring Becky.

"Yep, I knowed it," he groaned to himself. "The godlovin' look of a Callum."

"Callum?" Becky gasped.

Dibbs stepped back a little, as if Becky's stare was too unnerving—even for him.

"Which Callum may ya be, then?" he asked, one hand clutching the flask and the other reaching deep inside a dusty black trouser pocket. As if to steady at least one shaking leg.

"Daughter to Josephine Callum."

"Ah…." His mouth hung open. Teeth black from tar and decay, chin stubbly in coarse bristles of black and gray dapple.

Becky's own fascination was growing as she, in turn, studied Dibbs. As a young man, she was thinking, he must have been handsome. She didn't know why, but his presence had changed her mood, and suddenly she was seeing raw: a young Dibbs, the matted greasy hair streaked with gray suddenly jet-black and wavy, combed in a wave behind his ear. His eyes clear and sharp, a breathtaking blue with an impish twinkle; cheeks smooth where the wrinkled craters sank so deep they hid his dimples.

The man she saw was sprightly, and sober: laughing and dashing through the woods…in a white shirt.

She could barely stutter, "You've met my mother?"

Dibbs answered, "Josey?"

"When?"

"Long time back, 'n the parish days."

Dibbs at the parish: tall and lean, wearing a black frock and white collar; a graceful manner, a young priest looking more like Saint Sebastian kneeling at the alter of the Catholic Church. In Philipsburg. Becky was guessing, but her heart raced as if she'd just solved the biggest mystery of her mother's life.

"You mean…a Catholic parish?"

"Yep, but as ya may find it hard to believe—"

"A priest?"

Dibbs chuckled, and then winked at Becky as if she did, after all, share his secret.

"The nearer the church, the farther from God!" he whispered. "Bishop Lancelot Andrewes, if this 'ol stinkin' corpse remembers right."

Ben began to whine, "Mommy, l wanna go," as Becky waited for Dibbs to recover from a sudden fit of coughing.

"How did you meet my mother, then?" she asked, impatient to know more.

"No more prayin' now—jes pool," he replied. "Ya bet a dollar, and I'll oblige!"

It hit Becky then: that night of spying at Denton's, and the men joking over Dibbs's dollar bet.

"You know my husband," she added, hoping to encourage his confidence. "Trooper Dawson?"

Dibbs frowned. "Dawson? Sweet Josey's daughter is yerself, and yerself Mrs. Dawson? Damn!"

Becky nodded, but the news seemed to make Dibbs even more suspicious and confused. He stood there mumbling what sounded like complete gibberish, until Becky finally gave up. She'd have to wait. Think of a way to get him to talk sense.

Did he really know her mother? And was he telling the truth about being a priest? Becky was sure she'd caught him, once or twice—speaking in proper English.

As she reluctantly turned away and led an impatient Ben down the street toward home, she nevertheless resolved to try again, when she got the chance. Like next Tuesday.

*

I just can't concentrate on the economics. The freckled boy drifts back to where he belongs, in that other world beyond, and now I'm wishing my roommate, Lowie, was here. She's a good distraction. Completely the opposite of me. A real head-turner when it comes to attracting people's attention. Any people. She's never lonely. Lowie, a real gem: oozing with beauty and intelligence. I'm probably in love with her myself.

But she doesn't hang around here much.

Our apartment is cheaply furnished and cramped. But me, I'm always here. It's safer. Keeps me out of the even bigger shit. I mean, I used to go out just as much as she does, but I'm tired of it now. Looking high and low for nutbags. Nothing comes. Just an endless procession of people who don't have the eyes. Nope. Either they're fooling me, or I'm fooling myself.

And Lowie, I'm not sure. In a way, she's still a mystery, too.

I flip through the textbook again. Go straight to the interesting bit—pages 735-742—the glossy section of photos taken in the Thirties. I take a closer look: workers on strike during the Depression; a Chicago warehouse being smashed up; a bunch of pot-bellied New York Prohibition agents; a winding trail of dead-pan bread-line faces, Baltimore; farmers in Iowa standing like scarecrows in the dust; and finally a miner's riot in Pittsburgh.

I'm thinking—wait—wasn't my grandad killed in this very same riot? A strikebreaker's riot. In 1930, in Pittsburgh. I stare at the crowds in the picture: the angry miners in a skirmish of sticks and stone, the rearing horses, the fire and smoke and overturned trucks. I can almost hear the roar of chaos and fear; the clamor and crush of police, pressing in.

And I *know*. I look, and I don't see him there. No, it doesn't *feel* like the ghost of my grandad is standing behind that picture. I close my eyes, and the curtain opens to a different scene. There's trees; well no, it's more like woods, and Clem's running. *Is* it Clem? I'm not sure, just a glimpse of someone in uniform running—or rather staggering—through the woods. It makes me swear on my life that it's true, and I'm not mistaken: Clem was somewhere else. No matter what I've been told, my grandad wasn't there—not at that riot in Pittsburgh.

At some point Lowie walks in and I'm still bent over the book, twisting the ring around my finger and muttering "Oh my God, I'm sure of it now—my grandad wasn't killed in Pittsburgh. No, and Grandma knew it too. He was never there!"

Chapter Nine

The Drink

That's right, Lowie comes in and finds me talking out loud to myself, in a kind of trance, and I don't have to explain.

Instead, she puts her arm around me and gently takes my hand. Closes the reference book and asks if she can help. I tell her no, I just need to phone my dad. Find out as much as I can about the facts surrounding my grandad's death in Pittsburgh.

"You're all right then, Nina?"

"Fine, really." I'm shaking, but after a few minutes, I settle down.

She waits until I feel good and ready to slacken my hold on her hand. "I'm here, you know," she says, when I let go. "For anything."

"I know."

I'm really glad about that. Thankful.

Lowie still looks concerned, but smiling (rather sheepishly), I head for the sanctity of my own bedroom.

Lying on my bed, though, I feel like I'm ready to explode. The sensation of Lowie's fingers still warm in my hand, and the Pittsburgh photo such a shock, I'm scared. I'm thinking, is all this real? But Lowie, *she's* real. I listen for the reassuring proof of her presence—the sound of footsteps in the hall.

I hear a knock on my bedroom door.

"Nina?"

"Yeah?"

"Would you like to have a drink with me? I feel like getting drunk tonight."

"Well…I was just about to hit the sack," I stammer. "But all right. Sure. OK." I'm flabbergasted, but extremely amazed. She's never asked me before. But tonight's a strange night. All round. Getting drunk suddenly seems like one hell of a good idea.

"Where are we going?" I ask.

"Let's stay here. I've got some vodka."

I follow her into the kitchenette, where she rummages through her side of the cupboard, looking for this vodka. Out comes a large bottle of Vladamir's, which she kisses, sets on the counter, and unscrews.

At the same time she's smiling like an elf sharing a trick—with that impish curl in the corner of her mouth.

"Nina, I bet you don't even like vodka."

"You're right."

"But I'm going to make you a drink you'll like. You'll see."

She's wearing a black ribbed scoop neck T-shirt, under a pair of dungarees. Not the most flattering outfit for a female to wear, but when the upper bib billows out like hammock, holding those generous breasts, and a slim waist is cinched in by a red silk scarf wound like a necklace, it's as enticing as any fashion feature in *Vogue*. That is, on Lowie.

"We'll need a big bowl," she says.

Not that it matters we don't have one. She simply pops out for a minute and borrows one from next door. I just stand there and wait as the vodka is poured into an enormous stainless steel basin, exactly like the kind you find in the university canteens.

Half the bottle sloshes in, and a gallon of orange juice and cranberry that has mysteriously found its way inside the fridge.

"Are we drinking all that?" I ask.

"I'm not sure," Lowie answers, cutting an apple into slices. "But if we want to, it will be here!"

She throws in the apples, then spots my bananas on top of the fridge, so those go in too. Plus a stray orange. We carry the basin and glasses into her bedroom, and put it all on the floor.

Her room is a mess. She's an artist, with an artist's pile of sketchbooks, clothes and charcoal pencils to push aside before we can sprawl out next to the punch—legs extended and propped up against her sagging, cluttered bed.

She stirs the punch with her fingers, swirling the chunks of fruit and ice cubes until they slosh over the top. My task is to pick out some music. I decide on Lou Reed, as everything else looks unfamiliar. She hums along with "Walk On the Wild Side" as she hands me a glass, and our first drink together begins.

"I don't ask questions," she says, in the gap between albums. "If you want to explain something to me, you'll explain it. Right?"

I nod.

After the fourth or fifth serving—munching bits of saturated fruit—we look at each other and smile. It's as if Lowie has known all along what I've been hiding, and why I don't talk much. This impression puts me completely at ease. Something about sipping her punch and sitting on the floor with her, and I'm feeling much better, like it's real.

"It's good, this way. The vodka," I say.

"Well," Lowie replies, "there are some nights when you've got to drink tequila…you know those nights…and other nights are for Jack Daniels…or a thick, icy daiquiri."

"And vodka?"

"You tell me."

I think for a minute. "There are some nights," I say, "like tonight, when you've got to dull the pain. Tequila is too feisty. Whiskey is—too comfy, and warm. But vodka, it fits. Vodka's tough, a lonely person's drink. And you're disguising it, with punch."

Nodding, Lowie serves herself another glass, and holds it up. "Go on."

"I don't think you planned to drink vodka tonight—or spend the evening with me. You're killing time, waiting for somebody else. The one who I'm filling in for."

"You're right."

"Easy guess."

"But I'm glad he didn't show."

"You are now—but you're drunk on vodka."

Lowie laughs. "So are you!"

"I bet he's more miserable than we are," I insist, slurring the 'miserable' so it sounds rather silly. So I gulp, and articulate my next comment slowly. "Besides, I can't believe you'd *ever* be stood up by *any* guy."

Maybe Lowie has her nutbags, too, I'm thinking. But if she does, there's still this little voice warning me to keep my distance. I don't know why. I just don't think I'd ever tell her about Kurt, for example.

I mean, compared to Lowie, my disappointments are pretty mediocre. To begin with, there aren't that many. Kurt and I split apart just as abruptly as we came together. He asked someone else to the Senior Prom, but of course at that point I didn't mind. I think her name was Susie: another D-cup with long legs, keen on becoming a receiver for his next touchdown.

"But you know," Lowie adds after a pause, "the only thing you can *really* depend on, with guys, is their sex drive."

Laughing, we apparently agree on that.

Though I'm not sure if Lowie knows the other feeling. Not with those eyes, irises like a cat's, light green with a gray crisscross so distinctive it's almost spooky. Deceptive eyes and dusty brown eyelashes long enough to defy mascara; nose, kitten-petite; lips, thin and impishly turning up at the corners. With matching dimples. A bewitching smile.

I wonder. Would she understand how with Kurt I might have lost something far more important than my virginity? But I guess (as far as sex goes) I could argue it was better than nothing. At least I felt ready for college. Better prepared.

Or was I?

You can wonder.

At UCLA, maybe a dozen scuzzy disappointments my first year, half a dozen the second year, and three or four last year. But Lowie's had loads more experience, and apparently her physical passion isn't restricted to males, or the missionary position.

I've never asked her point blank for the details.

We've been thrown together as roommates this year by chance, and it takes time to get acquainted. All I know is what she's admitted in joking asides or little snippets of confession on the rare occasions she happens to be around. Most of Lowie's eating, sleeping, and studying is carried out on the sly.

I can't help but wonder why she cuts her hair short, like a man's. Straight at the top and sticking up, the lower half falling just below her ears, in strands that suddenly switch to a more feminine look—a layered shag.

Maybe she knows, catching my gaze and turning her head so I can admire the curling tendrils like playful fingers brushing her neck.

I mean, what does it feel like, only five foot two, and figure-perfect from your head to your toes? Having that kind of body: melon breasts, tiny waist and ballerina legs? Always looking sexy, even in white T-shirts and cut-off jeans?

Because Lowie's got brains too. High I-Q, she went to a gifted child's school and yet here she is, at UCLA, majoring in Art. Rebelling in every way and making me wish I could act like her, like a true bohemian.

"Believe it," Lowie says. "I've been stood up."

"Nope," I answer. "Not by any guy."

"Ah, Nina, but Geoff, he isn't any guy," Lowie replies. "So maybe you're right. Geoff is an entity unto himself. When he does show up, you'll see what I mean."

"I hope to meet him, then."

"I'd like to know what you think," Lowie half mumbles. She almost seems embarrassed. "You strike me as the psychic type. Well…aren't you?"

"What makes you say that?"

"I don't know. I'm not sure."

I don't say it, but I'm not sure, either.

Yet it's becoming clearer each time. Like right now: lying in bed, and despite the vodka, the curtain behind my eyes slowly opens…to find Becky.

*

In the darkness, she lay in her bed and listened. Was Clem sleeping? No sound from his bed, not even breathing. But the room, the air, felt charged. The black space above her head was vibrating; she was seeing raw—a dense cloud of half-invisible particles, all dancing in front of her eyes.

Why was her heart beating so fast? Why should she ache like this, in suspense? For nothing had changed, nothing was different about tonight. Yet it had to be something—even if only the seething, swirling energy of her own imagination.

Eventually, across the room, Clem's blankets rustled. Softly. While the dense, dancing air kept silent with anticipation.

She didn't dare speak, but surely Clem was awake. Still, no further movement and so quiet she wondered if he was dreaming that deep. Or holding his breath.

She waited. Eyes opened wide and staring up into the darkness with an excruciating desire to cry. Or scream. Anything, to cut through those restless specks and particles flying in every direction, filling every space of the rigid room.

"Clem?"

The whisper was her voice. But yet, as if her lips had opened—made that sound—of their own accord.

Ashamed, Becky slithered down, further, under the covers. How could she go on like this? Saying nothing? Wanting him back and yet vowing to keep her will, her pride, intact? The whisper was a sign of defeat.

Please let him be asleep, she was thinking. Please let it pass, and let me sleep, and stop feeling this…tense…suspension…in the air…

Becky's hands beneath the blankets cupped her breasts, as a man might caress. She pressed her lips against the pillow, and gently pressed thigh against thigh, feeling the warm comfort of her own body.

During the long stillness that followed, it felt as if nothing on earth would ease her torment.

But then, how long before it happened? The floorboards creaked, and suddenly Clem was there beside her.

In the utter darkness, his hands catching her head and sweeping her mouth with his lips. Softly at first, but harder as he sensed her matching relief.

As if time had turned back to the woods: wrenching clothes aside and aching to lose all sense of sense.

Who would deny it? Even now, to be blessed by the fire. And reclaimed.

Clem slipped under the covers and his bare skin touched hers, pressing lightly to relish every inch of her curving contours. The silence, growing deeper: fingers nestled in her crotch and lips skimming throat, nipples, belly; the moist trails of his tongue connecting every nerve ending as the fingers groped. Rested. Pulsated. Absorbed her rhythm.

The only sensation that, for Becky, was the ultimate of touch: mind melting into skin. This was raw. Part of life's dance, hidden in subtle strokes and the swell of passion. An endless tango of sweat, blood and emotion—where smiles come together for an instant and arms fling through the haze, closing the gaps.

She had no other measure, from Clem. But wasn't this enough? His physical touch?

And he'd come back. Abandoned *his* stubborn pride to remind her. Like he'd said, this was the core. This kind of surrender was all he could offer, as proof of his love for her, and love for the raw which bound them together. To talk about other things—no. That, he simply wasn't able or willing to do.

"Becky, Becky…why can't we live…fer this?" he whispered.

She couldn't answer. Felt a choking sob of relief rise in her throat, while his gentle, probing hands dispelled the years of neglect. Gradually, slowly, savoring the pulse of his penis resting deep in the softness of her womb; holding it there, there, there, until the smooth, subtle ripples of that pulse bulged and surged.

Burst.

A dim glow of dawn was seeping through the crack in the curtains, when Becky finally spoke.

"Clem?"

"No goin' to sleep, then?"

"No—can you sleep?"

"Not yet."

"So, do you forgive me?"

"You can tell that, I reckon."

Clem was still holding Becky tight, his arms wrapped around her waist, chin resting on her shoulder.

"Don't you think I can help? At least, talking a little bit, Clem, that might ease the burden."

"It's already come out," he said. "Some."

"You can't hide pain and frustration," Becky added. "But surely you can tell me why. Why does it have to be so secret?"

"It's best to been keepin' you outta this, Becky. The lesser you know, the safer you are."

"You're working with bootleggers, then."

"Yep."

"But you don't like what you're doing."

"Nope. What I been doin', it's against the law, but I ain't got no choice. Stuck like mole in one end of a hole. Me, and just about everybody I know."

"And there's bootleg at Denton's?"

"Tons of crates, all high quality whiskey, comin' from Ohio, through a syndicate the Mayor hisself supports."

"I saw you drinking the stuff…"

"Becky, just trust me. Nothin' goes the same as back home. Nobody here brews their own liquor. It's handy 'n cheap, rollin' outta trucks. Sewed up, big time. Liquor banned and nobody wantin' it that way—not even the people who started it up to begin with."

"Then everyone's breaking the law? What's the use?"

"There's good liquor, 'n bad. Honest runners, 'n crooks. Alls I'm tryin' to do is keep the real criminals outta town. At least, Denton's whiskey ain't gonna kill folks. Drink the bad stuff, full of wood alcohol—and you go blind, or crazy, or worse."

Clem sighed. He obviously wasn't finished, and his words hadn't come easy. They tumbled out slow, and careful. But something was pushing him to go on, despite the difficulties and his own misgivings.

"But now we've got bad stuff comin' in from somewhere else," he went on, "and it's gettin' serious. I've been tryin' to ketch these people through their runners. I've been sniffin' out the trail of poison."

"But something awful has happened. Today. Hasn't it?"

"There was this boy, he was jes a youngster, runnin' liquor to keep from starvin' and no way should it have happened…and Becky…I'm responsible. Oh I can still hardly believe it…but he's dead…and it's all my fault, damn it!"

Clem could hardly speak now. Hoarsely, he mumbled,

"This boy, me and him was friends. I coaxed him into workin' fer us. Least I thought he was workin' fer us, till this mornin' when we found him shot in the head, body tossed in the river next ta Woodmill Bridge."

Clem sighed, and held Becky even tighter. "I 'spect he was killed cuz he found out where the rival gang's hidin' their bad liquor, 'n told somebody. I can't figger who the boy tol, cuz it warn't me. I sure as hell wanna know but he didn't let out a peep to me."

"I don't understand. Why blame yourself?"

"He wouldn't have gone lookin' for trouble, if it weren't fer me. I paid him to snoop, and that's what he did. Only who got to him first? Either or, 'n never you mind, he was keen to help. Me treatin' him like a son, promisin' to keep him safe, so's he can end up dead. And fer what?"

And for once, Becky felt completely out of her depth. She could offer no words, no means of comfort.

"Poor little fella, that boy wasn't killed just fer laughs," Clem muttered. "He messed with hoodlums, and they ain't foolin' round. They got guns, 'n they're usin' them. But if I's right, I keep thinkin', and the boy fessed to somebody, why ain't that somebody tellin'? Makes me wonder which one of us is a traitor."

Becky shivered.

Clem shook his head. "So now you know," he said, "that's why I ain't been willin' to talk. Bad enough, I'm in it. So why go wiping yer own mind, Becky, with dirt not fit fer your boots?"

Becky nodded, tears swelling in her eyes. No, there was nothing she could do; and the frantic specks, once again, started to swirl above her head. A whole new army bouncing and crashing against the ceiling.

Chapter Ten

Dibbs

I stop by my dad's office in the faculty wing after my last lecture, and tell him I'm coming home for the weekend.

"Fine," he nods. "Good. Meet me here at six."

Walking back to my apartment, I'm glad it's only an hour's drive to get there.

It's the same white stucco house we first moved into, in the San Fernando Valley. It hasn't changed much in the last five years. Though now there's a pool. An aqua-tiled kidney-shaped affair, with a cement walk running clean around it. No weeds to pull, no grass to mow. No smell of open fields, rotting bark, sticky pollen. Nothing like that here. The neighborhoods in Southern California have a chlorinated, fabricated almost no-nothing smell. And if you do have room—after the pool—to grow anything, it's probably a clump of cactus, a row of dwarf palm, or a few skeletal bushes.

Teddy, the youngest, he's supposed to clean this pool, but there's hardly time—between high school, football and surfing. Jeff, he joined the Marines. We hardly ever see him, training on a Base somewhere in Louisiana.

So my mother, she'll be glad to see me. I don't spend more than a weekend a month at home (which she can't understand), but that's just enough to please and not quite enough to start any major arguments.

After grabbing a bag of books and clothes, I go back to the campus and meet my dad, and we're both sitting in his Land Rover, not saying much. Just watching the traffic mount and pile into the usual jams, heading for Highway 101.

I decide not to ask him about Grandad until after dinner. He'll be easier to talk to then, after his three Manhattans.

"Classes going OK?"

"Just fine, dad."

"I've seen so many promising students suddenly blow it, their last year. Either they get too cocky, or lazy—I'm not sure which—and think they can slide and bullshit their way through the last lap."

"I know what you mean."

We finally pick up some speed on the freeway, heading down the big hill into the Valley. But as usual, a brown strip of smog ruins the view.

"Anything new in the boyfriend department?"

"No."

"Not even Robert Redford?"

"Dad, cut it out."

"You can't even take a joke anymore."

"Sorry."

"So what's wrong with the guys at UCLA?"

"Nothing."

He throws me a side-glance, a familiar scowl, and gives up.

We've been through it all before. So I switch on the radio.

My mother cooks pork chops for dinner and Ben rushes off to the movies. I volunteer to make the coffee, and it's now I remember it's April.

"Didn't Grandma die in April?" I say, emptying the grounds from the previous filter.

"The eighteenth, wasn't it?" my dad replies.

"That's right," from my mother.

"So many years ago already," I sigh. "It's hard to believe, even now."

"The house and land, we've got to sell—you know—can't put it off forever," grumbles my dad. "The front porch is already falling to pieces. Who's going to pay for major renovation? I wish my brother would make up his mind!"

"Where did she get the money for all that, anyway?"

I ask. "How many acres? Ten, twelve? And the house, built to order, that must have cost a pretty penny."

"She saved," answers my dad. "But first, you've got to open a Savings Account, which I keep telling you to do, Nina—"

"Plus, she paid for you and Ben to go to college…and she never went out and worked, did she?"

"I should think you'd be able to figure that one out. Go on, get the calculator. Aren't you supposed to be a Finance major?"

"Dad, I'm just asking. I mean, why don't you like me talking about Grandma? You're always so vague when I ask you things."

"You should have asked her. She had a great memory."

"I know. But I didn't. So I'm asking you."

"Well, there aren't any bank statements going back that far. If there were, they were all destroyed by a fire in the attic, in 1938."

"A fire," I repeat. "So what year was it, when Grandad died in that fire in Pittsburgh?"

"I was six, so it must have been…1933."

I pass my dad his coffee and try to keep my hand, my voice, steady. "Do you remember that day? Anything? Anything at all, about what happened?"

"He was only six," my mom cuts in.

"No," my dad answers, "nothing except waking up, early in the morning, and hearing a loud knock on the door. Voices downstairs. So I stood at the top of the landing. Looked down. The door open, mother standing there, next to a Trooper. He had his hat off. Talking. Then she slammed the door in his face."

"She wouldn't let him in?"

"No, she slammed the door so hard it scared me. I think that's what made me cry."

My dad stares straight at me, hoping he's said enough. His eyes are questioning and they look uncomfortable, but not in any pain. It's so long ago....

"She never let another Trooper in the house after that," he adds, after a pause. "Guess I don't blame her. But she was too hard on the Force. They raised money, too, a fund for his surviving family. But she wouldn't take it. The Captain himself couldn't get her to take it."

"Boy," I mutter. "Talk about bitter."

"Three other Policeman were killed in that riot," my dad mumbles, "but my mother—your grandma—treated Clem's death as if it were the greatest improbability on earth."

"Death can feel like that," I hear myself say. "Can't it?"

My dad throws me his sideways glance.

I hesitate, but decide my last question can't wait.

"Do you think Grandma ever wondered if he was really dead? Since they never *did* find his body—"

"If the thought ever crossed her mind, she never said. No, that's ridiculous. She wasn't that crazy."

"So why did she go to Pittsburgh afterwards, looking for proof?"

"I never said she went there for proof," says my dad.

"Anyone have room for pie?" asks my mom, as she clears away the mess.

Well, that settles it.

Nobody refuses.

*

Several Tuesdays had passed, in fact, with no sign of Dibbs. But today Becky was restless and decided it was time to go looking. Bleary-eyed from lack of sleep, she fed and dressed the boys for the morning's outing. Andrew was escorted to school and, breaking the routine on a Thursday, she and Ben turned the corner. No promise of any cookie, and bound for Main Street.

Preoccupied with thoughts of Clem's confession the night before, Becky almost forgot to bring her basket.

Even in the early hours of morning he'd reluctantly left her side to wash and shave. Dress. Curse an early shift. Then, at five-o'clock and half asleep, she heard the front door open and close; minutes later only to be coming back. At the door, again, and stomping up the stairs; standing there, hands on his hips, smiling at her disheveled mane of hair, her naked shoulders. In full uniform, Trooper's eyes inspecting the crumpled sheets and suddenly turning, his riding boots bashing against the other bed. Kicking and shoving it, inch by inch, till it slid and scraped its way across the floor, to rest against hers. And without a word, marching out again.

Ben pulled at her arm. "Mommy, you go too fast!"

"Sorry, my love." She stopped for a minute to concentrate on the present and re-tie his shoe.

"Ben, look. See the robin over there? He's getting his dinner. And what does he eat?"

"Worms! Yuck!"

A beak digging, Becky was thinking, on instinct. So what did she hope to achieve, with these new insights into Clem's covert behavior? Could she blame him, after all, for wanting to keep some things buried? Perhaps Clem's mind needed a life of its own, separate from her. For if he couldn't be her equal intellectually, what was left? At least he had pride in his work; felt equal, if not admired, in that department.

Though Becky wasn't about to abandon her instincts to delve deeper, if they urged her on. Clem's love couldn't stop those, especially with regard to Dibbs. Dibbs, and the way he looked at her.

"Ben, why don't we go to the park?" she asked her son, still deep in thought as they sauntered past the Town Hall.

"Yes, mommy!"

Past Denton's, and no sign of Dibbs. Past the bank, and the Post Office, to the Square. Where a patch of trees and grass offered Ben a spot to play, and Becky a wooden bench to sit and watch.

Cool, but pleasant and sunny that morning in April.

The Square was deserted, the daffodils pale and limp in their final breath of bloom. Becky retrieved a blue rubber ball from her basket and tossed it across the grass. Ben, arms waving, shrieked with glee as he raced to fetch it back.

Inevitably Ben grew tired of this game, but not before Becky had spotted her man. Creeping out from the alley past Jasper Street, and slowly making his way to the Town Hall. Then stopping to sit at the bottom of the Town Hall steps.

"Come, bring me the ball." She suddenly swung an unsuspecting Ben up on her hip, and although he was rather heavy, carted both wriggling son, ball, and wicker basket across the street.

Breathless, she reached the steps and startled both the pigeons and the bum.

"Good morning," she huffed. "Would you mind if we sit here too?"

"God forbid, now here's a switch," he answered.

"I hoped I might see you again."

Dibbs squinted his eyes suspiciously at Becky as she sat down, put the basket by her side, and Ben in her lap.

"Ya hoped?" he asked. "Beware, fer hope deferr'd maketh the heart sick."

"Proverbs Thirteen," Becky replied, with a reassuring smile.

"Correct, but yer the sapphire lady!" he exclaimed, chapped lips breaking into a rather gruesome smile as he suddenly remembered.

"Waking the jewels in my turban," Becky reminded him.

"Yep, yessirre," Dibbs muttered, reaching into his pocket. "Now I's the one hoping ya don't mind if I—"

"Go right ahead," said Becky. "What have you got there—whiskey?"

"I perfer ta call it tea, perfumed ta my taste," Dibbs chuckled.

"Would you mind if I tried a sip?"

"Whoa now, why ya keep switchin' on me?"

"Switching?"

"Here!" Suddenly speechless for a change, Dibbs thrust the flask at Becky. He shook his head, as if he wasn't convinced he was awake. Or half sober.

Becky raised the flask to her lips and took a big gulp. The liquid burned in her mouth, but a warm soothing sensation slipped down her throat. Sank deep inside her belly. Snuggled there.

"Now that's a fine tea," she said, careful not to cough. "For times like this."

"Between woken hours," added Dibbs.

Now Becky was certain they both were speaking of the same thing. So I'm right, she was thinking, and Dibbs knows all about seeing raw, just as Saul's jewel awakes on his turban, giving the king courage and power.

She adjusted Ben a little, who was falling asleep in her lap. Now or never, she was thinking. This was the perfect moment.

"I'm grateful. Just one more sip? You won't tell on me, now will you?"

Dibbs' laugh was such a cackle, it turned the heads of a few people walking down the street. But no one was near enough to hear their conversation.

"Being Clem's wife," Becky reminded him, "I must say I can't complain his taking some for himself. So why shouldn't I?"

"Lord! Can you really be Josey's?" Dibbs exclaimed.

"From the bowels of a woman who scorned all liquor? Who rebuked as unblessed, the inordinate cup of the lecherous Devil?"

She'd had enough. Becky leaned over and gripped Dibb's arm.

"You're a smart man," she insisted. "You can talk properly. You've been educated. Once, you were a priest. You knew my mother. So why be hiding it?"

"The drink," he groaned. "O God, that men should put an enemy in their mouths to steal away their brains!"

"Please, won't you tell me how you know my mother?"

"Have you any Shakespeare?" he asked.

"Yes, yes!"

"Then you have all the answers."

Becky was losing her patience. Dibbs, on the other hand, seemed to relax. He winked, and then put his finger to his lips. "Wait," he said. "Don't go. Let me hold the boy, and I'll lift the shroud."

A strange request, with eyes moist, and haggard, yet still defiant. Sharp, deep blue eyes. A spark, under a haze of body stench; of cheap tobacco and stale liquor.

Becky carefully slid Ben over, resting his head on Dibbs's chest. Fast asleep, Ben lightly wiggled as he settled, but seemed comfortable enough in this new position.

"He's a fine boy," Dibbs muttered, staring at the round, chubby cheeks. An angel's face, serene in innocent slumber. "As fine as the boy I hoped to be raising with Josey. Could I stop loving her the way I did? Was it such a sin to think God had released me—to love—like He intended?

"So you loved her?"

"Such tender, fragile fingers, touching my frock. She, trembling on her knees to pin the hem, in the back chamber of the Church. In that chamber, hot waves of terror gripped at the seams of my soul. Ripped them clean apart. And she was only sixteen." Dibbs rubbed his mouth and swallowed. "A mender of Christian socks."

"My mother sewed for you?"

"She saved me," answered Dibbs, "from a Catholic Hell. The day I followed her out of the church, to the back of the Yew Grove. Ah, the spot still burns in my mind, yet it was wet, and raining, her arms around my neck…"

Dibbs handed his flask to Becky. "So you want to know, do you? Listen to the songs of the Bible. Many waters cannot quench love, neither can the floods drown it."

"Did you…leave her with child?"

"I swear on my life, no child, no child, no child," he chanted, squeezing Ben.

"Shall I take him?" Becky said. "We'll have to be getting home."

"He's yours, the child! It's yours, the ring! I see it!" Dibbs exclaimed. "But I can't see, no, not when there's no light—to see—why sweet Josey tossed it aside!"

"I know," Becky said, easing Ben off his lap. "Please, hush. It's so long ago, but I'm glad you told me."

So all this could explain why her mother hated Catholics! Becky frantically tried to piece Dibb's fragments together.

"But what happened between you?" she asked him.

"Tossed aside!" Dibbs repeated. "No hope, no light! I broke my vows, I won't say another word."

A man was approaching now and he looked concerned. Becky rose and set the flask next to Dibbs.

"Clem's havin' his sapphire lady. She's back!" Dibbs' voice boomed even louder as he sank back into his native slang. "Bless ya! Kin a priest bless, even if he knows nothin' of blood 'n bliss? No, fer how kin a priest be knowed if he's fooled?"

The man, relieved, watched Becky lift Ben to his feet. She nodded to him as she passed, leading her drowsy toddler away. Only then did she realize the man was Denton.

Dibbs let her go, but he hadn't finished. His last words still ringing in her ears as she turned the corner.

"—I bless ya, Becky, child, 'n Josey Callum! Me!

I've blessed! I've bled! I've touched! I've kissed the feet of holy fire, 'n spilled my seed 'crost a graveyard!"

*

He's got sharp blue eyes. So sharp and fierce I catch my breath. Just for a second. In surprise. His eyes so intense, they're fierce and gentle at the same time. A paradox. Piercing right through me.

But because of his clothes, his hair, I think he's got the wrong address. At first. Clothes hanging from his limbs like tattered rags off barbed wire. A pinkish T-shirt that might be faded red, full of holes. Baggy cotton drawstring trousers, thrashed and stretched and streaked with remnants of grass. Splodges of grease. Pleats of dust. And his hair, longer than mine: a sun-bleached blond, and tied in rubber band. A chiseled, weathered, Nordic-type face. Gold stud earring in his left lobe.

I notice all this in a matter of seconds. Standing at the front door of the apartment.

He mutters, "Lowie here?" and lowers his eyes. He keeps them lowered. Except for that first second, when the sharp blue windows briefly let me in.

"Yes," I answer, and let him pass, even though it's one in the morning.

It's got to be him. Or at least, I'm thinking, it sure as heck better be Geoff who I'm letting sneak down the hall like a thief in the night. And who doesn't even bother to knock before slipping into Lowie's bedroom.

Chapter Eleven

The Dance

I'm sitting with Lowie on the decrepit couch that came with the place, tasting another concoction of punch and I'm wondering what on earth next.

She's having people over. Here. Here, where she never likes to be—a box-hole of books piled high and riddled with trails of printed paper. Cubicle Number 32 of the Oleander Apartment Complex, complete with cracks in the walls, rickety cushionless chairs, a pair of soggy chipboard tables, and a threadbare couch. And me.

I wonder if Geoff is coming. But I haven't asked. Nor have I asked what happened a week ago, when he appeared like a thief in the night. Lowie hasn't mentioned it. Maybe there's nothing to tell. There weren't any sounds through the wall. Just a few muffled whispers. Then utter silence. They were real quiet. And the next morning there wasn't a trace of him left, when I got up. But still, something in his eyes—so blue, so sharp—remains. As clear as a bell.

"How many have you invited?" I venture to ask. She's borrowed the basin again—so it could be two, or twenty.

"Ten or twelve, maybe. Could be. I guess I should have warned you." Lowie smiles, brushing her hand over her cropped auburn crown. "But you know…It's better this way—last minute things."

"Oh I don't mind," I reply. And I don't.

It's nice to see how lovely Lowie can look when she's having people round. Tonight, I'm part of the audience, and she's pacing the narrow catwalk between the couch and kitchenette wearing a lycra turquoise shift. Barefoot, with silver spears dangling off her ears. Peeping through the smooth, snake-like strands of hair laced with glitter.

I nervously finger my own mop, a thick curly brown mass held in check by a ponytail (so far, the elastic ribbon has managed to stay in place).

"And tonight it's rum," I announce, ceremoniously unwrapping a stack of plastic glasses.

"Dark Myers and Dr. Pepper," Lowie adds, staring hypnotically into the basin. "Deep, smooth, rum. A sweaty punch. Dark and lush like a tropical paradise."

She gets up to fetch the ice, and suddenly mutters over her shoulder, "plus, Geoff really likes rum," as if it's an afterthought.

"Oh, I see." Question answered.

"So what do you think of him, Nina?" She's still rummaging inside the fridge.

Now how could I answer that, after a few seconds at the front door at one in the morning?

But I do. "He's different," I admit without any hesitation. "I like him."

And she doesn't make it any more difficult by asking me why.

While the next minute the doorbell rings and Lowie moves to the door to greet her first guest. I can hear a male voice exclaim "I'm the first one here? Good!" followed by laughter and scuffling noises.

I rush to the kitchenette to busy myself. Crackers, Doritos, cheese dip, carrots and celery spilling out of their containers onto plates. More rings on the doorbell before I've finished; five or six guys spilling over the couch, dipping into the punch.

"This is Nina, my roommate." Lowie introduces me as I scoot in and land the food by the basin.

The music is turned up. Suddenly I'm surrounded by Lowie's friends. Mostly male, mainly art students. Lowie is dazzling them all. She's holding long, intimate conversations despite the noise, her lips pressing against eager ears, gesturing with occasional sweeps of her arms, smiles and laughs bewitching in every slight inflection and subtle innuendo.

I watch from a corner, drinking several rums to fortify myself while the mixture of alcohol, pounding music and chaotic conversation begins to lull me into a fuzzy stupor.

Drunken faces leer towards mine. Some even attempt a friendly "What's your name again?" or "What's your major?" or "Why don't you dance?" I don't know why, but I rebuff with short replies and they drift away.

I think maybe I'm too busy thinking, waiting, watching for the moment when Geoff shows up. Lowie must be too—even more so—but you'd never know it. Not even when I catch her spotting him, like I do, entering the room and leaning against the nearest wall.

It's been hours, and we're all completely smashed.

Sure, I'm just as drunk but through the hazy screen, the wild laughter, blaring speakers and twirling limbs, I can see Geoff in the background. He's watching Lowie. His lips set in a soft, half-mocking grin as he squats against the wall. Stays right where he is, rolling his own smoke, and keeping a low profile.

I don't know why, of all people, he affects me the way he does. Really gut wrenching, this is. I can barely stand it. Take Robby, and a hundred million times over, and that's what it feels like. But why? Just because he comes across as different? So I'm hoping for a chance to talk to him. That'll do it. Burst the illusion right open. I'm willing to test it. Yes I am. Rip open the nutbag and get a good look at what's inside.

But there's something else going on here that's stopping me. Something nasty, I'm thinking. Cheap. And false. It stinks. Hangs in the air like scuzz.

No, I don't like it one bit, watching Lowie flirt. I don't even think she likes it—igniting desire, gushing sex, lavishing foreplay on whoever's handy—except the one guy she really wants. What's she doing, for God's sake? Punishing him for arriving so late?

I just can't understand why she's playing this game. Not with Geoff, who isn't fooled or impressed or even jealous. I can see that. I can see it the minute I squeeze past the dancers toward the punch; pour myself another glass; catch his gaze; blush; smile; cringe; hug my drink; hover past.

He looks amused.

I push my way back to the opposite corner, determined to confront Lowie. She's still dancing but I'm so drunk I don't care.

"Lowie!" I shout in her ear, "Geoff's here."

"I know," she answers.

Of course she knows! "Aren't you going to—?"

But she frowns at me, eyes glazed and lips pursed as if to say "Shut up, and don't judge me now."

I feel dizzy and stagger out of the way. A wave of nausea rising up from my stomach and filling my throat with a sick, sick, disgusting fountain about to…

I just make it to the bathroom but my vomit misses the toilet bowl, and feeling like an ugly, helpless blob of flesh I gag and convulse on the floor. The stench, the lumpy brown mess dripping down my thighs and making a mess on the tiles—I grip the bowl and thrust my head over the rim. There's more to come.

Vomit dribbling down my chin, I cough up more, groaning and sobbing with disgust.

Shit, shit, shit just let me die and end it now, I'm wishing to God, staring into the bowl, and the temptation grows: cursing the tears streaming down my cheeks, swirling through scuzz toward utter obliteration. Anything, to escape this hell. To be free of this planet.

After spewing what seems like buckets of lumpy brown-green gunge, I stop for a moment with a long tendril of spittle hanging from my mouth. Swinging like a masticated jellyfish through a fishing net. Suddenly I wonder if my grandma is watching; and if she is, would she let me go? For how can I carry on wearing her precious jewel, sunk so low—giving up so early?

But someone's here now, kneeling beside me and grabbing my shoulders, shaking them. Shaking me. It's hard to focus but past the bowl I see knees below, slipping on the vomit. I feel arms pressing my sticky, oozing blouse away from the toilet and up higher so I have no choice. I have to face this outside being, this human voice.

"Stop now, it's all right. Everything's going to be all right."

It's Lowie. She's hugging me. Running her fingers across my sweaty brow, smearing my sick all over her dress.

"I know what it's like," she's saying, "but it'll pass. I'll stay with you. Right here, like this, until it does."

She calmly wipes my chin with some tissue, and locks the door.

*

At the Mayor's Annual Policeman's Ball, Becky stood in front of the bathroom mirror, and wondered why she had this strange feeling someone else was looking back at her. Or was it simply the ghost of her true self, etched by her own gaze into the glass? A young woman. Soft brown eyes, round cheeks, rosy lips, thick brown hair, body plump and generous with the fairest of flesh. A humble Venus: sweet, soft and gentle. Smiling back at her, like a cream statue on velvet.

She adjusted the lace net around her bun. Checked that the clasp on her mock-pearl necklace was still positioned at the back of her neck. Then she pulled her corselet down—just slightly—to smooth the wrinkles, and looked again.

This time only Becky gazed back, wearing a low-cut velvet gown in green, with gray fur trim at the ends—neck—wrist—bottom hem, held by loose sash dangling off the hips. Clem had insisted she buy herself a new dress befitting the occasion, though she'd used her own pocket money to buy the pearl necklace. The necklace, plucked from the same mahogany jewel case at the shop with the sapphire ring.

Just for this very occasion, the Policeman's Ball, which she was enjoying tonight. Taking a brief escape from the dancing to powder her nose in the Mayor's luxurious bathroom.

She found it hard to leave the mirror. Spellbound, almost, by a strange urge to close her eyes and let the ghostly image possess her. But when she did so, the feeling changed, and the vision wasn't pleasant. The young woman emerging out of the darkness had wet hair, plastered in sweat, and her eyes were red and swollen; her breasts, covered in vomit. Sweat, tears, and vomit, all dripping down her naked white limbs to her ankles.

Becky opened her eyes and rushed out the door. She instantly put the image from her mind as the drone of voices, clinking of crystal, and strings waltzing a quartet drifted down the hall.

"Mrs. Dawson, may I have the pleasure of the next dance?" As soon as she reappeared, Denton crossed the ballroom floor and took her arm.

"If it truly pleases you," she answered.

Waiting by her side for the last number to finish, Becky wondered why Denton had asked. This short, stout man whom she hardly knew, with a big nose and a big mouth. Who for some reason she didn't like, or trust.

"Dibbs, he's an interesting character, isn't he?"

Denton smiled, his stubby fingers stroking his moustache. "He doesn't always speak sense, but it was kind of you to talk to him yesterday."

"He makes more sense," Becky replied, "if you take the time to listen."

"Yes...I suppose you know his sad story?"

"Sad story?"

"...Hmmmm...yes...such a talented young priest, brought down in his prime. A victim, really, of the miserable laws of church and state, and one hysterical wretch."

"Oh?"

"Indeed, it happened in your home town, I believe. Philipsburg? Though long before you were born. I assumed you knew."

"No, I don't know the story."

"Well then, back in 1906, a priest known as Simon Biddle was accused of raping a young girl. She testified against him, said he was drunk and ripped her clothes off, right there in the Churchyard. But Simon fled and they never found him. Defrocked himself, you might say. Changed his name to Dibbs, but some of us know who he really is."

"He told you?"

"Why not? It's of no consequence to me."

"No, but what makes you imply he didn't actually rape this hysterical wretch, as you call her? Was her sworn testimony that unreliable?"

Denton's smirk was annoying Becky. He obviously knew who this girl was, so why didn't he confess as much?

"You can't trust any female," he said. "I don't mean to offend, but it's true. Just ask any married man and he'd have to admit he sometimes feels accused of the same—by his own wife."

Furious, Becky nevertheless bit her lip and let Denton lead her across the floor. For Clem was watching and looked relieved that his wife, despite it all, was trying to be sociable with Denton. Denton, the wetter than wet Dry Goods man whom she assumed was Clem's bootleg partner, as well as a good friend.

"We're all indebted to Dibbs," Denton went on as he took her hand. "He's a good man, when he's half sober. He runs errands for me. Clem uses him too. But of course, I'd never tell Clem what I've just told you."

"But why not?" Becky asked, her voice calm but cheeks turning red.

Denton laughed. And using the dance as an excuse to pull Becky closer to his burly chest, he said, "I think it's better this way, don't you?"

Chapter Twelve

Geoff

The clock-tower bells are ringing for nine o'clock and I'm legging it across the campus green, trying to get to Stocks and Bonds on time. Unfortunately I'm not doing so well on this particular course, so I'm determined to attend this morning's lecture—despite a pounding head.

Besides, I'm hoping the outside air might help. Jesus. When the alarm went off, not only did I wake up with a hangover—but I was naked. Jesus. Naked. I can't remember how I got that way, but I assume Lowie had managed to drag me out of the bathroom at some point and put me to bed. While this morning, groaning my way into some clothes and creeping out of my room—I had to face the chaos and stench of the evening's remains. With Lowie's hasty scribble taped to the fridge: "Gone for the weekend. See you Monday."

But having made it this far, I feel better. And for some weird reason I'm glad I didn't flush my head down the toilet. Now why is that? I'm wondering why, since after last night it's fairly obvious Lowie is a bitch. I feel like I'm drowning in the scuzz; and the only person who can really help me now has been dead for five years. But—Lowie did appear at the crucial moment like a perfect angel and proved she could be a true friend. She can't be all bitch. I mean, even despite the scuzz, there's still hope. Thanks to that, and a morning in May that's as balmy and fresh as a bar of soap—I'm ready to carry on.

So I slacken my pace: choose to ignore the chimes.

It's worth taking in, this moment. So bright and sunny, fellow students weaving smoothly through the green: some somber, some smiling, some swishing past on bicycles. And the morning air so still, with the birds singing content, in happy tweets. Sounds of Eden, and such a pleasant mix of changing color: a rainbow of garments, a bank of iceplant blooming violet, and roses, pink and white, as I reach the verge. The earthy smell of bark and leaves; the dapple in the shade; the way the grass greens the green and cushions my steps like a salutary sponge.

Really good. Even the grass. I stop for a minute, and stoop down to touch this grass, which suddenly catches my attention in a new way. I'm transfixed almost, as if it's the most amazing thing on earth. Each green blade of the carpet an integral part, I'm thinking. Each tiny shoot born to rise, cleave, sway, fall, smash and survive as a whole: surpass the deluge of indifferent feet.

Then I carefully push a tuft of blades aside, as if I might find a tiny pile of black pellets hiding underneath. Deer droppings. As soon as I realize what I'm doing, it hits me. One instinctive gesture, and suddenly I'm sure. I'm seeing and feeling like Becky. And that's it: that's what she wanted me to have all along. Not just the ring, but a way of experiencing life as the most exquisite and beautiful nutbag of all.

I'm so enthralled by this discovery I've made with the grass that I veer off course and cut a detour though the middle of the lawn. I'm still smiling to myself when I get half way across, and notice someone else is doing the same thing. Cutting through the middle—from the opposite side. Smiling. Muscular legs striding in long leaps, blond hair bouncing slightly off shoulders, traversing the lawn in a kind of walking dance.

Getting closer, I see this person's got the same fair hair, broad shoulders and chiseled features, the same stern expression, same mouth, same pinched lips tweaked in Cheshire smile—as Geoff.

I find it hard to believe it's him, in decent jeans and a clean white cotton T-shirt, and ever harder to imagine he's slowing down because it's me.

But why not? And he does. He stops. So I stop. We stand there for a minute. In silence, acknowledging this weird coincidence, on a brilliant morning in May. Facing each other on the green.

Oh, and my face—and the way I'm feeling about the grass—I don't know what expression it turns.

He's got this grin. It doesn't change.

I start to wonder if I should say something.

Yes, better say something. Say something quick.

"Hello."

"Hello." He looks straight in my eyes. "Nina, right?"

"Right." I look straight in his eyes. I'm thinking so sharp, so blue, it's impossible. I can't, but I have to. I've got to say something more—before the feeling goes.

But instead I stick my hand in my pocket. Grab at the first object handy—something—anything—and I'm doing it before I even realize what I'm doing.

"Want a piece of gum?"

"Sure."

It's like my heart's swelled so big it's pushed everything into a 'distant mode' and I'm watching a slow-motion movie. It takes ages for seconds to happen. To realize: yes, the action is mine, and I've offered Geoff a piece of gum. I have. I've got it in my hand. And Geoff, he's said 'sure.' Which means this me in the movie should be making the necessary moves to give him some.

Now what is going on?

Because Geoff's still grinning, and he looks at me like he knows I don't really want to offer him a piece of gum; knows it's a feeble excuse for a simple hello which is actually a million miles away from what I really want to say.

Still. He waits while I fumble, fumble, to open the pack. Pull out a stick and reach out, arm slightly shaking, as if it's in the throes of some life-and-death task.

In slow motion. My hands, my arm, they can't help it.

But he's patient. He lowers his clear blue gaze to follow my trembling hand—and slowly, slowly, he takes the gum from my fingers. The way he takes the gum…the way he takes it…tells me he knows this instant has nothing to do with two students on their way to class, who happen to meet and exchange a piece of gum.

No. He looks into my eyes, and takes with such tender care what I've offered, that I know I'll never, ever, forget this moment.

"Nice seeing you…got to be off," he mutters, closing his hand so the gum rests inside his fist.

I nod, smiling.

Such tender care.

I watch him go. A flame, aflame, a star, a beacon of the universe. All wrapped up in some flimsy silver paper.

*

Clem's eyes gleamed in the semi-darkness as he held Becky close—undressing her after the Ball.

"I was doin' this all night," he mumbled, pressing his mouth to the base of her neck, hands sliding across her waist and impatiently wrenching buttons.

"But there's no barn at the Mayor's," Becky whispered, as his fingers slid past the buttons and up through the ridge of her corselet.

“’N fer so long—” he reminded her, “No nothin’.”

Becky sighed, and let Clem the Trooper recede from her mind. For these were such gentle, reverent hands—just like the Clem she would always know, back at the farm. Still driven to consume her, like a ripe fruit too soft and sweet to grapple or rush: his touch slow, careful, deliberate. Till his fingers passed her navel and her dress sank to the floor.

She quivered with pleasure as he fell to his knees and caressed her in places that would take them both, deeper and deeper, back to the raw.

“It’s goin’ ta be over, soon,” Clem promised afterwards, twirling the pearls of Becky’s necklace—the only thing he had failed to remove in the heat of passion.

Becky lifted her head. “Over? What’s going to be over?”

“What I’m sayin’ is, there’s talk the Prohibition is comin’ to an end. This year. Looks pretty certain, to some politicians.”

“Thank God…”

“So you ken rest easy. It’s comin’ to an end, and when it’s over I’ve gotta plan.” Clem paused to clear his throat. “What might you think Becky, of gettin’ outta town? Buying a place up the valley, in the hills? Our own place, with some land ’n trees.”

“Oh yes! But could we afford it? We’d have to buy a horse and buggy too…or an automobile…”

“I been figurin’…’n I think it ken be done. Been savin’ some extra money, you see—” Clem mumbled.

“Extra money?”

“Yep. Some extra cash.”

“Extra cash,” Becky repeated. “You never mentioned it before. Where is it? In a separate bank account?”

“Nah, it’s cash. I’ve hid it. So’s you wouldn’t know. How’s I goin’ to keep it a surprise, otherwise?”

"It sounds fishy to me," Becky said. But her tone was gentle, and forgiving. "It's a wonderful surprise. But hiding money…knowing what I do, Clem, I'm just wondering if it's legal."

"Nothin's legal," said Clem. "If I'd a kept on bein' legal I'd be—nobody—by now. I'm tellin' you true, Becky. The cash is fer upholdin' the law as best I can, as things are."

"Is it payoffs, for bootlegging with Denton?"

"If you wanna put it like that. But gall darnit, Becky, the Captain hisself is takin' it too. You have to—or they don't trust you."

"Who's they?"

"It don't matter. Like I said, it's all gonna be over soon."

"You promise?"

"Yep, and just remember that if anythin' should happen to me, go straight to Bear's Creek—"

"Clem!"

"Hush! Just listen: go straight to the fork at Bear's Creek 'n you'll see a lonely ol' Oak tree. Just under this tree's a rock. That's where you'll find it."

"No, I won't have you talking like—"

"Just in case," Clem insisted, squeezing Becky hard and then giving her a little shake. "The last secret, 'n now you know. You gotta know."

"But it's making me scared—"

"Nah, don't be scared! You remember the boy killed for fessin' that I told you bout, that made me worry so much afore? Well that's all settled down just fine. The boy, well, it turns out he tol' that fool Dibbs. But Dibbs, bein' on a drinkin' binge, he clean forgot. Took him a few days to sleep it off…but he come to, today."

Clem stroked Becky's hair and softly chuckled. But she wasn't relieved to hear it. In fact, something in Clem's voice struck her as being very unsettled.

"So the boy told Dibbs who's selling the bad liquor, and where it is?"

"Yep, 'n tomorrow we're raidin' the place. To smash every last bottle of poison 'n put those heartless gun-slingers behind bars."

"But what if these gun-slingers know the boy might have fessed to someone, before they killed him?"

"Well that was clean ov'r a fortnight ago. Don't reckon they's expectin' us if we ain't come by now. Dibbs thinks they musta seen the boy spying on 'em, and went after the boy right quick. Though not quick 'nuff, as it turns out."

"And you believe what Dibbs says?"

"Yep…'n I swore on that boy's grave I'd get my hands on whoever…'n put these guys away…"

Becky bit her lip. Yet what reason would Dibbs have, to lie? And to Clem? The very same man who'd entrusted her with the knowledge of his own guilt and her mother's…

"Does Denton know about all this?" she asked.

"Denton? Yeah, 'a course." Clem answered. "He's a hard man on the outside, Becky, but he's the best 'n this business. He's honest. He's even offered to help us fix up a place. The one we're gonna buy with the stash, up in the hills, like I said…"

While Becky pulled the covers and snuggled close, shutting her eyes in the hopes of blotting it all out. All except her husband's love and the dream of a house closer to the mountains—with the evergreens.

*

The lecture hall is a stadium of listeners, rows and rows of chairs and faces that point toward the center and focus on the speaker.

I try. I dutifully jot down notes and join the orchestrated movement of two hundred pens, but with ears ringing from last night's hangover; eyes swabbed to a blur from a backlog of tears; heart pounding from a stick of gum. I do try, but I'm not convinced.

I'm sure I'm not the only one. Of course not. But who else wants to own up? You can sit here, like me (even without a hangover) and go through all the motions of choosing a major, attending college, expressing all sorts of intellectual know-it-all, and feel like you're getting somewhere. You can feel alive enough, just doing this. What I'm doing. It works pretty well, doesn't it? To fill the Void?

Or you can be a nomad, I'm thinking, and simply roam about the globe exploring new cultures, pursuing a non-career, and expressing all sorts of spiritual know-it-all. Though that's not really any better, is it? Either way, you're still trying to fill the Void.

So I'm having trouble focusing on Stocks and Bonds. I mean, what's the true value of Births and Deaths? Why should we invest in a life full of fraud, or a business doomed to fold? We can't guarantee a God. Just a Void. So what's the point of us humans having a brain that's aware of this Void? It doesn't add up. Why have we evolved equipped with a consciousness we'd rather ignore? Take learning, fame, or material success; take love, or crusading to make the world a better place; or simply finding a way to eat your next meal. All equally sufficient, it seems to me, as a way to invest. To create value. To exist.

But sitting in this lecture hall, I know that even though I'm here, or if I were somewhere else—reading or dreaming or actually doing it—this absurdity would still be. The Void will always remain. So why should I have any ambition for what I already know won't make me feel any better, or answer the big question? I mean, what's the true purpose of what I'm seeking?

The answer must be—to beat the Void. To really beat it. And the only time that ever happens, for me, is when I find comfort—transcendence—in sharing this awareness with someone who has eyes like me. It's a connection of feeling that instantly "owns up" and yet rejects our deepest fears. It's not a school of thought, or even a hope. It's a connection. A current. It works through us all, to defy the absurd. It's what I call a nutbag.

Jesus, what else do we have? To really beat the Void? To really cheat death? And yet we wallow in objects, in wealth, in flesh and bone. And it's never enough.

So that's been my ambition. To follow the nutbag, and tackle the Void. The diploma, prestige, money, pat on the back—all that's pretty low down on my list.

And I'm thinking it's time I wipe off the scuzz and tell my dad.

Next time he asks.

Chapter Thirteen

The Bridge

Clem must have left as quiet as a mouse. Becky awoke to the sound of Andrew's cries, just past seven. She was alone in bed, but not for long. Before she even sat up, Andrew's little hands were gripping the edge of the bed, waiting for her to lean over and haul him in beside her.

"Mommy mommy…"

His troubled face was streaked with tears. She kissed it and said, "It's all right. Now what's the matter? Did you have a bad dream? Don't you feel well?"

"My tummy hurts."

"Here's some medicine for it," she said, pressing her lips over the soft button of his belly.

"It still hurts!" he insisted, but broke into a fit of giggles as soon as Becky's tongue began to tickle.

"Is Ben still asleep?"

"Yes. I don't have to go to school, do I?"

"No, have you forgotten the day? It's Saturday. And with a tummy ache, you better stay in bed."

By ten o'clock Andrew felt fine, so Becky once again asked her neighbor Mrs. Hartley if she would mind coming over to watch the children. Just till lunchtime. Mrs. Hartley was pleased to oblige. A lonely widow in her sixties, she loved playing "the gran" for Becky's two little boys.

Becky thanked her again and again. Then raced out of the house—on another quest. This time, to the Dry Goods Store. To find Denton.

Her thoughts, her movements, all seemed to be happening in fast-motion. Time was running out. She could feel it pushing her into a state of panic. Though from the outside, who would have guessed? The same Becky, tall of stature and humble in dress, hair twisted firm in its bun, shoulders stiff under the shawl, and no hat. Striding like a queen, in sure steps, toward a successful day—starting with the shops.

But her feet carried her right past the Baker's and she disappeared inside the Hardware Entrance of the adjoining building. Denton's was a big shop with two stories and two ways to enter—not counting the door at the back.

The hardware aisles were narrow and crammed with goods. Boxes of nails, endless in size and length, seemed to whiz past her peripheral vision like spiked trenches of war. Then—boom—the space was clear and she knew Denton himself would surface, stationed behind the barrier at the far end. Leaning against the open counter in front, with shelves of cloth and ribbon behind. Denton's corner.

But no! There was no Denton.

"Can I help you?"

Becky confronted the even stouter and more repulsive figure, at that moment, than the man himself: his sister, Flora. Today of all days, sitting in his place.

"Is Mr. Denton here?"

"No. But I'm sure I ken help."

"No. Thanks, but—I'd like to know where he is.

Please."

"Don't know where he is."

"You must have some idea—"

"Nope. So what you want him fer?"

"Oh, nothing. It's all right. I'll come back later."

"You do that," Flora replied, smirking and crossing her chubby arms across her chest. "You're certain not to be wantin' what I ken find. I ken tell that much."

Becky turned and didn't even bother to answer. She marched out, wondering what on earth she *did* want Denton for. No, she didn't have a plan; didn't know what she dared to ask him for or even hoped to learn in return. It just seemed imperative to do something—fast. Not to wait, but face the mounting dread and ease the growing suspicion.

Next stop, she was standing in front of the Police Station. Just about to walk in when Sergeant Grimsby came out.

"Oh, hello Mrs. Dawson. Are you looking for Clem?"

"No—yes—I mean—he's not inside, is he?"

"Afraid not. His whole division's gone off, on a…well…it's a secret mission, really. Don't worry. I'm sure he'll be back for late supper."

"I sure hope so," Becky replied.

"You just keep that roast warm in the pot for him, now hear? Nice seeing you." And he smiled. Stepped around and left her standing there. Whistling a tune as he went.

Where to now? Becky scanned the Square: no sign of Dibbs, either. But then—wait—she spotted him. Wasn't that Dibbs coming out of the Second-Hand Shop? The next instant he'd already disappeared—down the side-alley. She raced ahead, but the shop was two blocks up, and by the time she got there, it was too late.

She decided to take the alley and follow Dibbs to God knows where. The alley was long, and narrow, and damp. The cobbles ended and the ground underfoot was basically back-door garbage; her boots getting wet and heavy from the filth.

But it finally ended and she found herself back out in the open, where George Street ran into the road leading to Ganger's Mill. The river itself could be seen in the distance, flowing gently through a vacant field.

And less than half a mile ahead, in a hunched stagger, a figure—who had to be Dibbs—was plowing his way through a path in the field. Heading for the bridge.

Becky ran. She knew if she hurried she could catch him before he crossed the river.

"Behold, this dreamer cometh," he said, as soon as he saw her approaching. "You know the verse?"

"Yes. In faith, I wish I could be like Joseph," Becky answered, "with his coat of many colors."

She felt rather foolish now, having caught Dibbs resting in the shade by the bridge with a large bottle of whiskey in his lap. He apparently was in no hurry and much too thirsty to settle for his customary flask.

"Ah, I thought so. And what brings you here?"

"Pity," she said. Though she hadn't planned to say it.

"He that hath pity upon the poor lendeth unto the Lord," quoted Dibbs.

"No, it's me," she said. "I'm the one in need of pity. Please, I'm hoping you can help me…"

"Calm yourself, I'm not goin' anywhere," he said in between burps. "Oh, excuse me. Now, what could be troublin' the heart of our precious sapphire lady? Sit yourself down. There. Now, is she feeling better?"

Becky nodded. He offered some whiskey, which, of course, she felt obliged to accept.

"I'm worried sick over Clem," she blurted, "and this business with the boy. The boy who was killed."

"I'm sick about the boy too," Dibbs replied. "A good lad, a wee monkey with the mind of a fox. That's why I keep comin' here. My penance! To pray for his soul, and his poor scrawny corpse, soggy and green with riverweed, floatin' right over there—just there. Can't you see it? And up here." Dibbs pointed to the brick arch above. "Look how his blood—his innocent blood—hangs o'r the end of this bridge!"

Just in case, Becky didn't look. Not at the bridge.

Instead, she gently put her hand on Dibb's sleeve. And catching his eyes in hers, she watched the reflecting orbs fill with tears.

"It's spill from the drink, so don't let it fool you," he mumbled.

"But you can't lie, not to the jewel," she insisted.

"No."

"Then is it true, that you told Clem exactly what the boy told you?"

"Not so true...."

"No?"

"Well, I didn't actually hear it from the boy first-hand. How he stumbled on their stakeout, switching Fed markers in the woods. Up near Highgrove Ridge. Or how he hid, so he didn't think they'd seen. That's what he said, but he told it to Denton. It was Denton told me, and I told Clem."

"But why didn't Denton tell Clem himself?"

"He said I'd be best to tell, and get some credit...said it's better this way."

"Better this way...." Becky almost choked on the words. Sounded just like...

"—I have ventured," Dibbs mumbled, "Like little wanton boys that swim on bladders, this many summers in a sea of glory—" And gazing into the river, he sobbed, "—but far beyond my depth."

"So you didn't tell Clem the whole truth, did you! Did you? And not a word about Denton asking you to tell him?"

"It's all in the bible, or Shakespeare," he answered.

"Speak plainly!" Becky entreated. "I will listen, I want to understand!"

"He paid me," Dibbs mumbled. "Paid me for being a friend to the boy, and Clem. Proverbs say there's a friend that sticketh closer than a brother, and I'd never harm neither. Never!"

"But you have!" Becky exclaimed, wringing her hands.

"Can't you see, Denton is using this deception to his own ends?"

"No harm done!" Dibbs insisted, but he covered his eyes and groaned. "But I needed the money, and can't think clear, not with the boy's blood still wet on the bridge!"

Becky could feel her own cold terror beginning to take hold and she began to shake. The next thing she knew, she was shaking Dibbs. Hard.

"We've got to *do* something!" she almost shrieked. "Dibbs, you've got to help! Help me now!"

Dibbs let her shake him.

Then, suddenly tossing the bottle into the river with one hand, and grabbing her arm with the other, he said, "Stop! Our paradise is lost! Listen: who overcomes by force, hath overcome but half his foe!"

Becky released him and Dibbs stood up.

"I've woken," he said, "and cast my bread upon the waters. Trust, and thou shalt find it again."

"But how?"

Dibbs rubbed his chin and muttered, "The Reverend…Reverend Goodman…Denton said he was payin' a call…yes! To that Jesus church…"

"Jesus-Our-Savior church?"

"—and Denton, when he paid me, he joked, called the Reverend a two-timing, two-faced Baptist…"

"But what does it matter?"

"His glee," said Dibbs. "True, he was boasting and bound for the church. Listen: the voice of the boy! He whispers: go to the Baptist church. His ghost points to the river. The river points to the church."

And creeping up the bank, Dibbs stumbled through the tall grass—in search of the path.

*

"Your hair is different."

That's what Geoff says, when I open the door.

"No ponytail," I reply. "That's all." But his comment cuts my composure into bits.

"Lowie here?"

"No." I shake my head.

Yet he still stands there—even so—as if I'll let him in. Again. Though it's only just past eight. While tonight of all nights, I've left my hair hanging loose. Completely unfettered and somewhat uncontrolled. Just for this.

Something else is different too, I'm thinking. Geoff's smile. It's weak. And forced.

"I should have called first," he mumbles.

I nod.

"So that's that."

"She's back Monday."

"Monday."

"Yes."

"And where's she gone?"

"I don't know."

"But I can guess."

"It doesn't mean—"

"—a thing? Ha!"

"Would you like to come in, have a beer before you go?"

I hadn't planned to say it, but all this time he's been looking down—at his feet—and now he lifts his eyes. Bitter blue, I notice. Bitter and hurt and resenting Lowie.

"Thanks."

I fetch two cans of Coors and he sits on the couch, sinking in the hole between the cushions. He's deep in thought as I set one on the floor, near his shabby leather sandals. Then I sit down too, on a folding chair.

Now we'll finally talk, I'm thinking. So I wait. Watch how he fingers the can between swigs, until he's twirling it empty on his knee.

"So," he almost smiles. "It's down to you a me. Auld Lange Syne."

I'm not sure what he means. But I've got my own way of putting things.

"She's in love with you," I blurt. "Lowie. I'm sure she is."

"But she has a strange way of showing it."

"And you don't?"

His blue eyes gleam with passion as he leans towards me—hands gripping his thighs. "At least I don't run off and sleep with other people," he mutters. In a voice so low and subtle, it could be an emotional plea. Or a cold sneer.

"It doesn't matter," I insist. "Can't you tell? She still loves you, so she's scared. She's scared of a love that's...that's...so...well, you know..."

"Crazy?"

I smile, feebly, and trembling in my own fear, I answer, "No, it's not crazy."

"You've got a better word?"

"Yes."

"Which is?"

Now I feel the urge to clam up. I can't believe we're diving in like this. So fast, and because of what? A lack of proper introduction?

"Go on, just say it."

I say it. "Well...you know...divine."

There's a pause, but Geoff doesn't flinch. "Ah, Nina. Not fit for mortals," he answers. "Let's stick to physical passion. I know exactly where it hurts. Lowie, she's the cause as well as the cure."

"Come on. I know as well as you do. She's more than a sex object."

"Then why doesn't she act like it?"

"Maybe she wants you to tell her how you feel."

"How I feel?" Geoff squeezes his empty beer can, watching me cringe at the sound. Slowly—crack, snap, pop, snap—he crushes it in his hand.

He's toying with me, I'm thinking. But I won't be a sucker for such dramatics.

"Women need to be told," I remind him.

"What for? Are words any proof?"

"No…" Now what do I say? "But…you could share some of your feelings…"

"Oh, you mean like how I despise her for making me want her every day? Or how I resent other men lusting over her body in the same way?"

"You know that's not what I mean."

"I'm hooked, but I'll be damned if I'm going to be chained, like a handy slave." Geoff raises his eyes and looks at me. "All the rest is fucking games."

I can't disagree. Nor can I defend Lowie. It all seems impossible to me, like the myth of a virgin nymph who slips through the arms of a Greek God.

"Is that it?" I ask. "Sex and fucking games?"

"No," he answers. "If it was, why would Geoff be drawn to Nina, and taking solace in her deep brown eyes?"

When the beer runs out, we walk to the corner store and Geoff buys a bottle of Bacardi. He asks the clerk for some rolling papers and I get the feeling we're about to carry on—from that piece of gum.

And it helps to smoke. We relax. Open up. Geoff admits he hates college and dresses like a bum because he's rich. Well, at least his parents are, and I wonder what his major is and he makes me guess. I take a stab at Religious Studies and he's fairly certain mine is English. So we're rolling on the floor, in stitches, over Economics and Political Sci.

"I never finish a semester," he adds. "I don't stick around long enough." He takes off his sandals and rubs his toes. "No cure for itchy feet."

It isn't long before he's asking if I've ever tried Acid. And I have to blush, and say no.

"I'm surprised," he answers, "but then Nina must be a lucky girl."

"Lucky?"

"Some of us need drugs to take trips."

"But what makes you think I've tripped?"

He chuckles. "This."

"This what?"

"This now, and this morning. Or have you forgotten?"

"So tell me what it's like—" I insist. I try to remember the sensations I get when the curtain opens, and I see Becky. "Does it make you feel invisible? Do objects melt into dancing specks, and merging rainbows? And then does time jump like a yo-yo, or completely lose its grip?"

"That's right," he says.

"And then, because everything around you looks so clear and vivid, you begin to think real life is the dream?"

"Who isn't dreaming?" laughs Geoff. "But no, I'm serious. Nina, it's there in your eyes."

"They say the eyes are the windows of the soul," I venture to add. "But what exactly do you mean, when you say it's in my eyes?"

Geoff seems amused I've even asked.

"Hmmm...that's tricky. Not easy to explain. But let's say life's like a bridge...one long walk across a suspension bridge. Yes? Picture in your mind, this long suspension bridge. Now. We're all human and we've all got to cross this shaky bridge. And below our feet, right beneath, is a deep gorge that's black and bottomless. The Great Abyss. Death. Non-being. Nothingness. If we look down, we're petrified. So some of us don't look down. Follow me?"

"Yep, so far."

"Then it's obvious, isn't it? Some of us close our eyes, cling to the side-ropes, and creep slowly to get across. Others find it easier to fix their gaze on the other side and rush headlong to the finish. There's several ways to get across."

"True—I suppose it's easier, and feels safer, if you don't look down."

"Right. But what if you do look down?"

"You might feel inclined to stand completely still. Or throw yourself off."

"Suicide, eh? But what if you don't jump? What happens then?"

"You get drunk?" I'm looking down at my hands now. At grandma's ring.

"And after that?" Geoff asks.

I'm stumped. "Probably keep going, but that won't stop you from looking down," I admit. "But why's that any better?"

"I'm not sure it is," Geoff answers. "But think about crossing the bridge that way. You'll pass lots of other people who never look down. You'll know who they are, because of their eyes. There's no reflection there, no hint of the deep abyss. But pass a person who knows, who's seen it like you—and there's hope.

"Hope?"

Geoff chuckles. "Why not hope, from someone who doesn't take acid, yet says there's a love...divine?"

He reaches over, smiling, and pulls me to the couch.

I'm not even sure if it's me—or Becky—who falls into his arms. Suddenly I'm there again, sliding down from the wagon and clinging to the power of touch. It's the same feeling: stroking his hair. Though his name is Geoff, and his blond mane feels like silk, and smells of earth, of musk, of marijuana. Resting my face against his, I'm cleaving my skin to the sun; his cheeks bright and hot as they brush against mine; we lie together and sigh, like lovers. But no, we're touching like ghosts. Passing our lips, our limbs, over boundaries that can't be real. Nothing feels solid.

I think we were here before. Ages and ages ago, when we already knew all there was to know, and it's made us so restless and tired. But we've found each other again. Beyond the corruption of body; embracing like kindred spirits. A brother and sister.

Parted from a distant heaven, and condemned to the here-and-now.

CHAPTER FOURTEEN

Denton

Jesus-Our-Savior was nestled in patch of trees, mostly pines, which could clearly be seen about a mile down river. An old stone church, it was, and for many years stood derelict—until the Baptists moved in.

Dibbs led the way. He assured Becky the path was a short cut, if you knew where to find a gap through the fence surrounding the Mill.

But the path was broken in places; they tramped across mud, clawed through bracken and tripped over rocks. Though in April, the wild undergrowth along the river was just beginning to emerge. Tiny green buds on the thorny hedges promised a new crop of blackberries, and small patches of yellow buttercups and dandelion poking through the grass would soon attract the bees.

Dibbs stopped for a moment to catch his breath, and Becky was glad he did. They both stood still, high on the bank near the Mill, and felt the clean, crisp caress of a mountain breeze as it passed through the valley.

While the Black River flowed like an overloaded barge, a sluggish conveyor heaving from the load relentlessly pouring off the mountains.

Pine branches, leaves, mulch and rock-ice debris made the water look as black as the rich forest soil.

Dibbs turned and said, "I've showed Clem this place. He's bringin' his boys here to fish, when they're old enough."

Becky nodded and wished for the day to come soon.

But then, staring across the River, Dibbs let out a horrible groan and fell to his knees. "Dear daughter of Josey forgive me," he wailed, "but I can't go on!"

Becky knelt beside him and tried to pull him up, but he held fast, clutching the ground like a obstinate child.

"Oh, how this Spring of love resembleth," he sang, "the uncertain glory of an April Day...which now shows all the beauty of the sun...and by and by...a cloud takes all away..."

"Come on!" she commanded.

"I need a drink!" he said, rubbing his lips. "I'm too shakin' wi'out it."

Becky pleaded, "Oh Dibbs, please get up."

"Forsaken for what? What does the Bible say?"

"The race is not to the swift, nor the battle to the strong."

"Ah, yes. But a cloud, a cloud takes all away!"

"Look," Becky said. "Can you see over there, where there's trees? That's the church—not far—and I can see a truck. I'm sure it's Denton's truck!"

Dibbs looked. Cursing under his breath, he sat there. Thinking.

"You shall go," he answered. "Run, and make haste. But hide. Pray listen. Listen and pray, as I have a plan. Conceal yourself near the place and I will follow. I will have words with Denton, and bait him with questions. He will answer, and if Denton's a traitor, we both shall hear."

"I'll go then."

"Go! But hide and wait for me!"

Becky nodded, then kissed Dibbs' hollow cheek—before she rushed away.

The trees hid her approach and the stone wall around the gravestones provided a stooping cover. It was Denton's truck, all right, parked in the rear: where the trees left off to grass, and a new building had been added to the original chapel. She slowly raised her head above the wall and read the inscription above the door: The New Advent Sunday School.

Crawling on her hands and knees, Becky crept behind the wall as far as she could go. She was concealed less than twenty feet from Denton's truck when she heard voices and the sound of boots crunching over gravel.

Then a bang: probably the door of Denton's truck.

Was he leaving? She held her breath.

"Fine, fine, it's done and settled then." Denton's voice, loud and gruff, cut through the silence. "No sense having a cellar like that go to waste."

"Dry as bone, to boot. Not many basements like it." Another man's voice, but much softer.

Denton laughed. "Guess we broke a few cobwebs but who's gonna notice? Reverend, I assure you these fellas are as good as their word. Your cup runneth over, eh?"

"I didn't expect this much," the Reverend replied.

"I'm almost choking myself," Denton answered. "And all I did was switch suppliers. Two hundred dollars a month for hiding a different brand of liquor. A lot of money, Reverend, to woo in a few more converts. And you'll have enough left over to build more pews, too."

"You can't be doing too bad yourself."

"Now you listen here…I may not be known for going to church, but it doesn't mean I'm not inclined toward helping those in need, with a bit of charity."

"Well thank you, Mr. Denton. God bless, and keep us all in peace."

"That's right. See you again, next month. Meanwhile, rest assured the night owl keeps his eye on things. Movements so quick 'n sneaky you'd swear it was mice."

"You've got the keys."

"Yep."

"Fine."

More feet crunching the gravel and suddenly, with a rumble, the truck's motor began to idle. Becky didn't dare look, but surely Dibbs had appeared—just in time. For the truck hadn't moved, and she could hear the gackles cawing up in the trees.

Then, the sharp clank of the motor's last turn as it wound down again.

"Dibbs you fool, you startled me!"

"Denton, you knave, you fooled me!"

"What's going on? Has something happened? Get in the truck, and we'll—"

"I ain't goin' nowhere," Dibbs insisted, "dead or livin', drunk or dry."

"Shhhsssh…I don't want the Reverend to hear us and—"

"I can be quiet," Dibbs said, audibly shaken but his words still ringing clear. "Ain't that why you trust me?"

"Yes, yes," Denton replied. "Now what's so urgent it can't wait?"

"I've been thinkin' and it don't sit right," Dibbs grumbled. "It ain't right if what I took was blood money."

"What?"

"Sure, it felt good, tellin' Clem what he wanted to know. I did, didn't I? I told him accordin' to the boy, the bad stuff's hidin' near Highgrove Ridge. But half sober, I'm thinkin'…why me? Why's Denton payin' someone else for the pleasure?"

"A mutual deal, Dibbs. Same as before."

"But I'm haunted by that bridge! And blood! It don't make sense. The boy wasn't that stupid to get himself seen by the racketeers…"

"Maybe not—"

"But he's been killed!"

"So they must have seen him, after all."

"Our boy, he was too smart to be that dumb."

"We all make mistakes," Denton sneered, his voice trailing off so Becky could hardly make it out. "Yep. Especially when we're too cocky."

"Naw…there's somethin' rotten in this, and three hundred dollars ain't enough," Dibbs sneered back. "Not if you're fixin' a new deal on the sly—with the racketeers and the Reverend."

Becky could hardly stand it now. She wanted to shout "yes, yes, he is!" to Dibbs, but she had promised. She'd have to wait…

"Well you can go to hell, Simon Biddle, you cocky cunt-lovin' priest!" Denton growled. "I've given you more than you deserve already."

"Give me the truth, and I'll leave be," Dibbs insisted. "Or I'll spook the Chapel, and scare your tipsy tit-suckin' teetotaler of a Reverend."

"Hang on," said Denton. "No sense getting ruffled over a bottle of split milk. Not when the next dairy's bringing you buckets of champagne."

"Does Clem know?"

"He'll never know, don't you see? When the boy fessed to me, I went straight there—to Highgrove Ridge. I made a deal with them."

"You snitched?"

"For a thousand dollars, and then another thousand, when I said I knew of a hideout—a damned safer place to hide their store. They had to act quick, too, with Clem hot on their trail."

"God almighty, I don't see," Dibbs groaned. "What's the use? Clem…he'll never switch sides…not to gangsters pushin' guns and foul liquor."

"Clem won't be any trouble," Denton muttered. "I'm taking care of him, and we'll be raking it in, ten times more than we ever were."

After a slight silence, Dibbs coughed, and by the sounds of it, spit on the ground. "Got a drink?" He chuckled, but it sounded hoarse. "I'm real thirsty 'n I left my bottle by the ghost."

"Have some of this. Now let's get going!"

But Dibbs paused, probably taking a few more swigs of Denton's liquor. "So it was you," he sputtered. "You killed the boy. Mighty clever."

"Now Dibbs, was it my fault he wouldn't fess to me, not until he sees a gun? Or lets himself get shot, and falls in the river when he ain't that fit to swim?"

"I reckon not," Dibbs replied. "Besides, I've taken the money, blood or no, 'n spent it already."

"So stop complaining," said Denton. "Now you know, and it's better this way."

Becky pressed her head against the crumbling stone wall, her body racked with grief and terror. But the cold, rigid surface couldn't hold her firm; the moss now wet with her tears; the grass uprooted in angry fistfuls.

What else could she do?

She could stand up. Be seen! And shout, "Dibbs! What about *you*? What makes you think Denton trusts *you* not to let the cat out of the bag?"

Which she did, letting out her words of rage in one long shriek.

Both men jumped and swung around to face her. Dibbs looked scared to death, but Denton's eyes betrayed no fear. Not even a flicker of dread. And in that instant Becky realized he had won.

"Get in the truck," Denton said, "both of you. I'll take you back to town—or wherever you want."

"Yes, you're going to take us to the Station," Becky answered, "and we're going *now*."

And just as they drove away, the Reverend came out. But Denton didn't look back, nor did he stop to explain why Dibbs and this woman, after causing such an uproar, should be hitching a ride in his truck.

"You're a despicable man." Becky leaned over Dibbs to sneer at Denton. "I always knew you couldn't be trusted."

"That's not giving much credit to your husband's sound judgment," Denton replied. "In his estimation, I'm as good as his best friend."

"I'd never do anything to hurt Clem," Dibbs whimpered. "No, no, no, not for all the money in the world."

As the truck rumbled past the factory, heading for town, Becky knew: it was too late, and whatever threats of justice or revenge she could throw at Denton now wouldn't stop what had already happened.

"You've killed Clem too, haven't you?" she shrieked.

"Nope, it wouldn't ever be me. How can it be? I'm his best friend, remember? Dear, dear Mrs. Dawson, I could never do that. Point and fire a gun into the face of a man who trusts me? I'm not *that* despicable."

"They'll be waitin' for him at Highgrove Ridge..." Dibbs mumbled. "The racketeers, they'll know he's comin'..."

But they were getting closer to the Police Station, and Becky snarled, "You won't get away with this, Denton."

He simply shrugged. "It's a shame, really, that Clem has never been quite as clever and intelligent as you. But then, you can't always have a marriage of equals, can you?"

"You're going to hang," Becky insisted. "And before you die, your vile tongue will throttle your vocal chords, and then you'll go straight to hell."

"I'm afraid you're wrong," Denton answered. He glanced over at Dibbs, sitting between them in a drunken stupor. "Who's going to listen to your story? The Captain? The Mayor? Or were you counting on the Judge? They're all part of this new deal, you see. You'll have a hard time finding someone who isn't stuffing his pockets with money from Highgrove Ridge."

Becky still refused to give in. "I'll go to the Feds, then," she answered.

Dibbs laughed. "They'll promise to look into it," he replied, "but the Feds happen to be pals with our gangsters from Chicago."

"They can't ignore reliable witnesses!" Becky exclaimed.

"You got witnesses?" Dibbs continued to chuckle. "Besides, you got any proof?" Denton looked over at Becky, and winked. "Are you counting on Dibbs, perhaps?"

Becky, completely rigid with rage at this point, nevertheless managed to bend over and shake her last vestige of hope. But Dibbs didn't respond.

"I'm dying," Dibbs mumbled. "A sword's carving the insides of my stomach…"

"He says he's dying." Denton's smug expression hadn't changed, not even as he parked the truck in front of the Station. "Fancy that. But they say it's lethal, boozin' on methanol."

Half unconscious, Dibbs' body was slumped in the seat and Becky had to pull him upright again. She would have to drag the old man from the truck.

"But Clem! If they haven't killed him he'll—"

"He won't say a word in hell, now will he, Mrs. Dawson? For if I go down, we all go, and he goes too. Just in case you've forgotten—Clem's rollin' in payoffs from similar endeavors. Or would you prefer to think of them as crimes? Like you do with me? Eh? It's a shame, I know, but there's nothin' a woman like you can do."

Becky was half out the truck, and burdened with a floundering Dibbs, when she struck.

Leaned over and with all her strength, and slapped Denton hard on the cheek.

"Mrs. Dawson."

"Yes, I'd like to have word with the Chief Inspector, please."

"He's not here right now."

"Then someone else—who can I speak to?"

"About what?"

"Getting an urgent message to my husband, Trooper Clem Dawson."

"I'm afraid there's just a few of us Policeman, and Dispatchers, on duty. Everyone else is away on special assignment."

"The whole unit?"

"Yes."

"Where?"

"Sorry Mrs. Dawson. You must understand. I'm not at liberty to say."

"At Highgrove Ridge?"

"Where?"

"Highgrove! Just tell me it isn't Highgrove!"

"I'm not at liberty...but look. Would you like to leave a message?"

"For who?"

"The Captain?"

"No, no I just want to get word to Clem. It's very, very urgent." She was vaguely aware the answers weren't going to be given—not when the questions were asked in a shriek.

"Is someone in the family ill?"

"That's it—yes—so I must get word," she said, lowering her voice. "Please, please let him know he's got to speak to me, right away."

"I'll make sure he's contacted, as soon as possible.

That's a promise."

"Please."

"Take it easy. I'll see about getting the word out. All right?"

"Thank you."

Becky turned and walked out, slamming the door behind her. The officer's frown was enough to convince her he wasn't about to radio the unit. Not when he could clearly see this ill family member out the window, lying prostrate on the Station steps. There was no mistaking that useless bag of bones known as Dibbs.

*

Mrs. Hartley was worried sick and hugged Becky with relief when she finally appeared.

"Don't you dare do that again," she exclaimed. "No call, and no knowledge of where you are!"

"Where's the boys?"

"Right here, makin' bridges with their blocks out back. It's been a fine day, so we've been playin' our games outside."

"Good. Thank you so much. I'm sorry I'm so late—"

"—but look at your torn skirt, and those muddy boots! My lord, where've you been?"

"Out by the river…it's a long story…but don't worry. I'm fine. I decided to visit the church, and pray, and I lost track of the time."

"Well I'll be off now. They've had their lunch, and a snack too, so don't let 'em fool you about bein' starved or nothin'."

Mrs. Hartley followed Becky out back, to say goodbye to the children and watch Becky greet them as if she'd been gone for weeks.

While Becky was hoping she wouldn't cry, or look as suspicious as Dibbs, who was waiting outside.

"Bye…"

"Bye bye, now"

When Mrs. Hartley left, Becky whispered to Andrew:

"I've got a surprise."

"You do?"

"We're having a visitor. He's a friend of Mummy's and Daddy's, but he's not well. He's got a tummy ache, so we're going to help him feel better."

"We are?"

"Yes. So you take Ben and watch me help him in."

What else could she do? Becky felt she owed something to Dibbs, who risked his life to help her, and face the terrible truth—of what he'd done.

Standing in the hall, Andrew and Ben were transfixed. Through the open front door came the ragged remnants of Dibbs, drenched with sweat and groaning with pain as he leaned on Becky for support. Yes, the boys looked shocked—but not frightened. Not by a blubbering scarecrow who collapsed in a filthy heap in the parlor—on the spotless, blue-and-brown patterned carpet.

"What's your name?" asked Andrew, bold as a magpie teasing a tail-twitching cat.

"My name's Simon," gasped Dibbs. Then, suddenly focusing his eyes on the curious son, he sobbed, "Simon, a disciple of the Lord…and the Lord is Love…young man…and don't you…ever…forget it."

*

I'm still awake, but Geoff—he's sleeping. We're spending the night on the couch. Like this. It's cramped, but it's not so strange. Only I can't sleep. I know I'll probably never get the chance to touch him quite like this again.

I'm quiet, though. I don't disturb his slumber, but wonder what it might be like to feel him skin on skin—without our clothes.

I'm thinking of Becky, too, as I breathe deep and find it hard to hold back the tears. Now it's my story, the wagon. And the ring, that's on my finger, though I often forget. But when I remember, like now, the feeling makes me slowly raise my hand to my face, and run the sapphire-circled diamond across my lips. I rub slowly. Tracing every facet in a dreamy echo of a kiss.

My grandma's eyes come back. The ring feels solid when it's pressed against my mouth. While now, more than ever, I'm surely close. She's close.

The air around the couch, in the darkness—is whirling. I must be drunk. But I'm not rum drunk. My mind is clear, my senses sharp. I have this urge to rise, and find her. Go and look—in the bathroom mirror.

The connection is now, I'm here safe in Geoff's arms. But it won't last: I know I'll have to let him go.

I still wonder, was it really my grandma, in the mirror that night, catching my moment of crisis? And there was Lowie, too, in the glass: pulling me out of my own stinking vomit.

Scuzz, scuzz, scuzz.

I know the scuzz is here, even now. It's choking Becky. But I can't see what it is. I can't sleep. I keep my eyes open, whisper to the ring: "I can feel it. Something went wrong. Let me see it happen."

CHAPTER FIFTEEN

The Betrayal

"So," my dad states, slumped back looking rather smug and comfortable in his black leather swivel chair. "This is it. The last four weeks of your last term."

My face is solemn, but I'm working hard to smooth the cracks. "I'm almost there," I promise.

"And you've done so well," my mother adds, brushing dog-hairs off the matching couch. "You'll graduate on the Dean's list, with honors."

"I only wish," my father goes on, "that you'd make some moves toward the job market. Put your name forward, send some letters out."

I nod, but feel this awful lump growing in my throat.

"I guess you think it's too early, but it's not," he says. "Now that we've spent all this money sending you to college, you've got to use it—use that diploma—to help you get ahead. Because I know you're not the type of girl who goes to college just to find a husband."

"Not that we're worried you won't find one," my mom cuts in, "...or think you shouldn't be satisfied with staying home and raising a family."

My dad ignores this. A pause: the chair emits a faint squeak as he leans forward and reaches for his drink. "Nina, I'm just wondering. As you haven't said a word to us, and we don't want to pressure you—but—what *are* you going to do, after college?"

I have a choice, now. I could cut the scuzz with my dad, like I promised myself I would, and see what happens. Or, I could chicken out. A decision that is made by simply opening my mouth and waiting to hear what comes out.

"Oh I suppose I'll go and maybe find a job downtown," I hear myself say. "In one of the LA skyscrapers, on the twenty-fifth floor. If that's where the jobs are."

"But what kind of employment will you seek?"

My mom bites her lip. She's obviously undecided.

"The kind that fills the void," I answer. Well, I'm trying.

"What do you have in mind?" quips my dad, who won't be flustered.

It's easy for him, I'm thinking. Ever since he was twelve years old he knew he wanted to be a maths and physics teacher. Then up, up, up, the predestined ladder, to Professor. To a PhD. To always know what he wants, and what comes next.

"Well Dad, I've been thinking about scouting the ads—say—for assistants to finance assistants. For Publishing Firms." That sounds good, and I'd only just thought of it.

"You always did like books," chirps my mom, encouraged by my answer.

"At any rate," my dad concludes, "until you do find something, you can always live with us."

"Whatever's best for you," adds my mother.

I nod. It's just not easy, talking straight. Not with parents. Yet I felt I had to rush away from Geoff, on a Sunday, just for this.

My mom decides it's time for bed and my dad grabs the TV guide. He's going to check the time for the late football game. I'm sure he wants to watch it so I hope it starts at ten. I sit tight. Half an hour means a second chance.

"Dad?"

"Yeah?"

"When's the game start?"

"Ten. Did you want to watch something?"

"No."

"Is there something else on your mind? That you want to discuss?"

"It wasn't me who wanted to discuss the future. That was you."

"Sorry. But I'm not a mind reader, Nina. I don't know what's bothering you. But something is, right?"

"I haven't been straight with you."

"No? What's happened, then? Are you pregnant?"

"*No*, it's not that. I'm just depressed. Confused. I've been having dreams. I can't sleep. It's got so bad I'm cutting classes. I can't even force myself to study."

"It'll pass. It's your last term. It's fatigue and nerves, like I warned you. Remember?"

"Dad? Would you forgive me? I mean, if I freaked out and didn't finish this term?"

"That won't happen," he says. "You're fine. You look fine to me. You're a Dawson, and Dawsons are tough. Now some parents, yes, they've got kids who are psycho mental cases. Or addicts. Or neurotics. Or maniac depressives. But as for you..." he smiles and shrugs, "...you just think too much."

I think he's trying to be funny and get me to laugh. But I do smile and realize he's probably right. Though that doesn't seem to explain the strange reoccurring visions.

"I keep having these dreams about Grandma," I try to explain. "These dreams...they're so vivid. And the strange thing is, I'm the one who's

Grandma. Whatever happens in the dreams, I'm feeling it as though I was her."

"That's not so unusual, is it?"

I want to say "it is if you're awake and simply closing your eyes" but I'm not going to tell him that. Not when he doesn't look ready or willing to hear it.

"I suppose not, but I've been wondering if they might go away—if I stopped being so curious about Grandma."

My dad frowns, but his tone is sympathetic. "So what's a father to do? What can I say, Nina? I guess it's not surprising she's left such an impression on you."

"But dad, you were her first son. And her favorite, am I right? The bond must have been pretty strong between you."

"Isn't that more a women's thing?" he replies. "If anything, at times I felt she smothered me with all that love. And I didn't have my dad..."

"No dad around," I finish, "to balance it off with a man's thing. Then I guess you had to fill the gap—and step in your dad's shoes? Maybe you felt a bit guilty, for taking his place. I think I would."

"I wouldn't call it guilt," he answers, rubbing his chin. "A lot of resentment, I suppose. My mother was a passionate, obstinate woman. I have to say I've always thought it ruined their marriage—almost drove my dad away. Then, in the worst way, he really did go."

"For ever..."

"Sure, Ben and I were too young to understand.

When she told me he'd been killed, I felt overwhelmed."

"Overwhelmed?"

"After my dad died, she went sort of crazy, and started what I'd call a crusade to fortify the family. Beginning with me. I can't say, Nina, if anyone deserves that kind of devotion. She was like a Diva, trying to mold an unsuitable protégé. And frankly, what's so good about all that love and passion? In my experience, it only messes things up."

"I know what you mean," is all I can muster.

"So Nina, you'll have to let her go. My mother—your grandma—is dead, and dreaming about her like she was some kind of saint isn't going to bring her back, OK?"

I'm glad he's opened up, so I smile and quickly move to his chair for a daughterly hug.

"OK."

We both relax.

"Dad? One more thing?"

"Yes?"

"Remember when you told about the morning the Trooper came, and told Grandma about Grandad—and how she slammed the door in his face?"

"I remember."

"Well, can you remember anything at all, about the day before?"

There's a half-sigh, half-groan: but he's thinking. I'm growing hot and slightly dizzy just waiting.

"I remember Mrs. Hartley, watching Ben and me play in the yard. I guess it stuck in my memory because the strange thing is, when mother come back, she had an old man with her," he says. "I'd never seen him before—this skinny, filthy, stinky old man—and he was sick. My mother dragged him in and laid him on the parlor couch. Big wide blue eyes he had, shiny as marbles. I remember that. I remember his name, too. It was Simon."

I close my eyes and whisper the name.

"Whatever happened after next, Nina, is a blank. Ben and I must have been sent to bed. This Simon wasn't there—the next morning. I forgot all about him, after that."

"Were his clothes old and torn, like rags?" I ask. "Was he wearing clumpy black coal-miner boots?"

Now my dad's had enough.

"He looked like bum, but my mother said he was a friend," he mutters. "Will that do? I'd like to turn the game on, if I may. Do you mind?"

"No, go ahead," I insist. "Or we'll both miss the kick-off."

And I sit and watch: waiting with eyes still closed. A few more seconds and the curtain opens even wider...there's Simon with his boots...and I'm holding fast to the image of Becky bending over the couch: wiping a frothy phlegm from the old man's chin.

*

Dibbs was seriously ill. He fought to stay conscious and kept coughing up bile. If he wasn't coughing, foam oozed from his mouth in tiny bubbles, like dirty soap being wrung from the folds of wet laundry.

Becky wanted to call a doctor, but Dibbs begged her to leave him be; begged with such heart-wrenching fervor that she couldn't do it.

"Please, just listen," he mumbled. "I'm past hope, but I'm reconciled to it. Denton knows...it's the bad stuff—the poison—that gets drinkers stiff. Thousands go stiff, go blind, go dead...all doomed...denatured...no...body...nobody's clean..."

"Dear God, isn't there something a doctor can do?"

"No, no, nobody's clean..." Dibbs gurgled and choked, as he struggled to speak: "Can't you see? I'm telling you, nobody *can* be clean."

"Lie still," Becky answered. "I know, please. Save your strength, and don't try to talk."

"When I was a priest, I kissed a Cardinal's ring," moaned Dibbs. "It's true, a Cardinal's ring is sapphire. Eyes azure...bluest sky...a hope divine...deep calleth unto deep..."

He winced in pain, but his eyes stayed open, focused on Becky's face.

"But I only felt touched by God...that moment my lips kissed Josey's...and yours...but I mean I only kissed your ring...the ring that's yours," he went on. "It's safe in the sole of my boot."

"My ring?"

"Take it…as a sign of faith, despite a misspent life that withers…and dies…for the love of your mother. Hold it close to your heart, as I hold you both."

"Do you mean the ring in the Second-Hand Shop?"

"…and the tent shook, for mighty Saul shuddered—and sparkles 'gan dart, from the jewels that woke…"

"Dibbs, Dibbs!" Becky was crying uncontrollably now, her tears falling drop by drop into the folds of Simon's tattered coat.

"Do you think Josey might have loved me?" he said, eyes searching Becky's for some sign of recognition.

"Oh yes, I'm sure she did," Becky answered, stroking his heaving chest.

"But how do you know?" he answered, staring at her with those blue, bloodshot eyes.

"Because I love you," Becky sobbed. "If I had met you as a young man, reciting your Shakespeare and looking at me with those eyes as you sometimes do—what choice would I have?"

"You would have lain with me, and not run away?"

Becky nodded. After all, she knew in her heart, now, that the young priest was as close as she'd ever come to finding the man in the white shirt; who had eyes like hers; who ran laughing through the woods. The man she'd always wished Clem could be.

"I often hoped…you were looking…past…the drink…" Dibbs muttered.

"Oh, but why oh why didn't Clem look past the money?" Becky wailed.

"Wine maketh merry…but money…answereth all things." Dibbs eyes, turning blood red and swollen, were half shut. But he opened them wider and said, "You must know how the money…that the money…I took from Denton…was only to buy you the Sapphire…"

Becky was silent: confused and bewildered.

"Ah, but the ring's…clean as an Angel," he whispered. "They say God created the angels from pure, bright gems. My blindness or greed can't tarnish its worth. So take it...take it...when I'm gone...I want you to...have..."

"Dibbs? Dibbs, please, can you help me understand? Is it true, that my mother betrayed you? Is that what you meant, when you said she tossed it aside? What made her reject your love? Accuse you of rape?"

"We both felt the heat...of holy fire," Dibbs answered. "But she suddenly shrank away, like a doe in the jaws of a wild beast...in a sudden terror...I withdrew...then spent my lust...on the ground..."

"I spilled my seed 'crost a graveyard—" Becky repeated the words she had remembered so well, but failed to understand.

"I saw fear in her eyes," he groaned. "She couldn't let go of her mind...and the feeling frightened her. As our fears do make us traitors..."

"So she testified against you, and hated all Catholics ever since—"

"A celibate Catholic...the devil in drink...was all to blame."

"But you weren't drunk, were you?"

Dibbs tried to chuckle, but coughed instead. "Not on your life, though I went straight to it after..."

But getting shorter of breath, he wasn't able to finish. "Do you think Clem forgives me?"

"I'm sure he does..."

"Then please...just...take off...my boots," he whispered.

And then he closed his eyes. While Becky ignored his jerking, twitching feet, and reached instead for his hands. Hands that turned limp and cold in her grasp.

*

"Are you asleep?"

"No." I open my eyes and suddenly realize where I am. At home. Me, Nina, sitting in front of the television. With my dad.

There's the muffled roar of a packed stadium, of chaos and shouting, and the high-pitched squeal of a commentator "—he's going—he's going for 10, 20—just look at him go—!"

"Touchdown!" My dad shouts.

I wait till it's over, and mutter, "I'm not really watching, Dad." But my heart's beating just as fast, and

I sit bolt upright. Rigid. Tense. Itching to tell him.

"Christ! It's about time!" he exclaims, his attentive gaze still glued to the screen and fixed on the replay.

I nod. And I know Simon's dead.

But I don't say a word. It was such a shock, to have the curtain open again—and right in the middle of a football game—finally discover who really gave Becky the sapphire ring.

I never would have guessed.

Yet who was this strange old man? And why should my dad believe me, if I described what I saw? I'm thinking, Becky didn't tell. She didn't tell a soul. And that was enough to convince me. Whoever Simon was, he had the eyes, and his misery ended when Becky took the ring.

So I say nothing to my dad except "goodnight" and go straight upstairs, to bed. But I won't sleep, I know that, not after seeing Simon die, and assuming Clem will surely follow. But how? I only know this: Becky was closing her eyes and feeling Clem gone even then.

Feeling him gone. Closed eyes, and sitting by the couch. Waiting for the night to pass. Here with the outer corpse of skin and bone, and the inner echo of Simon. And what's left. The filth and stench of some unwashed socks, caked with sweat and matted flakes of calloused skin, dried-out puss, grit and dust. The blisters binding them on, and like glue, closing the gaps from the holes. The socks hold fast to the scum.

But the ring drops out, just the same. Hidden in the sole of his boot—cushioned in the fold of one of his socks.

That's what I saw. Enough to send shudders down my spine; Simon's foul body, his haunting gaze, a voice that still whispers in my ears, saying, "Nobody's clean."

"All right," I groan. "Now please let me sleep!"

Rocking and moaning, beginning to cry; I pray; the whispers finally stop; but the night drags on. I stare at the clock. So tense and restless I feel the need for some air. So I creep downstairs and, gently unlocking the patio door, push it open. Just enough to pass through, and stand there. Inches away from the pool, looking up at the moon, which is only a sliver tonight, and a sporadic sprinkling of stars.

Even though it's chilly, I strip down. The water's warm. It feels good, dipping naked into the silence, and floating in my little sea. I'm enfolded. Caressed by an invisible host that covers me with an endless succession of kisses: smooth, wet, and effortlessly following my every move.

Smiling in the darkness, I listen to the soft rippling sound of my presence. The pool's content. I wonder if I, too, could just let it be. And stop trying to feel it through others, and pass it on with words.

Chapter Sixteen

Lowie

My mom and dad, they'll never believe it—and besides, I could be wrong. I could be wrong, and the truth isn't what I see. But my dad doesn't want to go feeling around for the truth. He doesn't trust feelings. So he doesn't want to know what it is that's making me have these dreams. And my mom, she doesn't like causing a fuss so she follows my dad. Why would either of them want to know how Grandma got the ring? If it didn't come from Grandad?

So I don't think I'll ever tell them. I mean, my dad doesn't even ask me how I knew the old man wore rags and miner's boots. Riding back in his Landrover Monday morning, though, I notice he's quiet. Thinking his own thoughts. Then he offers to help me write some of those letters. I say thanks, and when he drops me off just outside the campus, I rush off, pretending I've got a nine o'clock lecture. Well—I do, but I'm not going.

Instead I'm hoping to catch Lowie at the apartment before she skips off again. I don't think she has a Monday morning class, but I'm not taking my chances. It's quicker if you're coming and going on a bicycle, but I'm making good time with my long-legged, wide-strided trot.

When I burst in I almost trip on a pile of objects placed just inside the door. A little pile of boxes and bags, like the kind you put things in when you're getting ready to take them somewhere else.

"Lowie?"

"I'm here, Nina. Hey, where've you been?"

"I went home yesterday."

"Oh. What are you doing now?"

"Nothing."

I'm standing just outside her bedroom, which looks suspiciously over-messy this morning. As if she's been tearing it apart, looking for a needle in a haystack.

"What's going on?" I ask. "Have you lost an earring, or is it a shoe this time?"

"Could you help me out?" She's bending over a mountain of clothes strewn on the floor of her closet. "I think I've got some string somewhere, but I can't find it. Do you have any? Or how about some tape?"

"I've got tape—"

"Masking tape? I've got to wrap these paintings," she exclaims. "Vince will be here in an hour."

"Vince?"

"Yes, Vince. This guy I've just met who happens to be gorgeous and rich and runs an Art Gallery. In Malibu. He's got one in San Diego as well. That's where we're going—San Diego—and he's coming round to fetch me in less than an hour!"

Her paintings aren't ready, but she is. I notice the crinkled semi-transparence of her white muslin skirt, the splash of beige and lavender gracefully sweeping between her legs as she stoops. A band of thin silver bracelets chinking as she moves her wrists; adjusts a strap on her loose midriff top. She smells of sweet exotic citrus, and she's wearing make-up.

"Have you been…with him…all weekend?" I ask, as Lowie flings open a newspaper and lays out the pages, side by side.

"More or less," she replies. "Now would you mind, bringing that tape?"

I help her wrap each canvass. Twelve in all, and for the first time I get a close look at some of her work.

"This is my favorite," Lowie explains. "The only one that's framed. What do you think? Does it make any sense to you?"

I'm looking at men and women who mingle together: in a sketch that's wild and half-abstract, wriggling in blotches of purple and black. The background is blank. The figures are stark: their limbs intertwine, but the flow is distorted and tangled. To me, the faces look smudged and mean—almost ugly. But there's a kind of beauty behind them, like frantic moths. That's what I'm thinking: like little neurotic creatures that flit back and forth from the hell to the light.

"Do you think they're depressing? Or evil?" Lowie tilts her head and waits for my answer with those elfish green eyes.

"I wouldn't say evil…but rather…intriguing," I reply. "Depressing, but in a weird way—appealing."

"You're carefully choosing your words," Lowie adds. "But then I guess you always do, like Geoff."

Just hearing her mention his name is enough to make me blush. But I knew he'd come up. He had to.

"Lowie, I've been wanting to ask you about Geoff."

"What would you like to know?"

I gulp, and keep on wrapping, as I muster up the courage to say, "He was here, Saturday night."

"Oh? And what did he say?"

"Not that much…but Lowie…" I lower my voice so she knows I must really mean it. "Jesus, it's obvious, isn't it? How much he's in love with you—"

"Nina, I know you probably think I'm being really callous, but you haven't any idea what it's like."

"How…I mean why…I don't understand."

"Feel free to join the club," Lowie mutters. "What does he want, from a female? Who knows? There's moments when he's fantastic, but they never last for long. I keep thinking, what's going to happen—in the long run? And he knows how I love him. I always will—but what's the use, loving a guy like Geoff? A crazy nomad? He wanders, Nina. He comes and goes as he pleases, he disappears for weeks at a time, and expects you to wait like Penelope, in case he comes back. It goes on like this for months. Sometimes he doesn't even bother to phone, or write. Can you understand it? It just doesn't add up."

I notice her voice is real shaky—for once. She's trying hard to hide it, but I can tell. She's on the suspension bridge, and Geoff is wrenching her hands off the ropes. But she won't let go.

"Now I hurt so much…I want to hurt him. But it's no use. He'll never change."

"From what little he said to me Saturday night," I manage to utter, "I think he's been testing your doubts. If you want him to prove this kind of thing, you can't. I don't think you ever can. All you can do—is know, and believe."

"This kind of thing," Lowie answers, "isn't at all what I thought it would be."

"So you're running off with someone like Vince?"

"Nina, it's just got to end. I know what I'm doing is right. At least Vince…he'll never wound my pride…or drive me nuts…like Geoff does."

"Though he won't have the passion—"

"For what!" Lowie exclaims. "If it's not all for me?"

"It messes things up, doesn't it?" I can't help but add. In my dad's own words.

Though I think she knows, even so, how I disagree.

"Nina? What are you thinking?"

We've finished wrapping her paintings and Lowie's stacking them near the pile by the door.

I'm so full of emotion I can't answer.

"You know, just in case you're not sure, I don't mind if you start seeing Geoff," Lowie mumbles, averting her eyes and shaking her head. "I'm going to move on. Stay with Vince at his place in Malibu. So whatever happens now—between you—that's up to you."

She hands me the tape and because our eyes still don't meet, I'm not sure if she really means it. But what made her say it? So, I'm thinking, I haven't been wrong after all. We are alike, and Lowie realizes I could easily fall for Geoff too.

But is she trying to warn me I could end up like her?

"It's not like that," I insist. "No. What I want—is for us—to stay close."

"Me too," Lowie nods. "Don't worry, I'll keep in touch."

I'm so confused and Lowie's frantic rush to pack, her hasty departure with Vince, puts a damper on everything. Just when I was about to open up completely and tell her the things I've held off from telling her before. Like how close I *do* feel—to her. Or how rare it is, people with certain eyes. Yes, and how unspoken pacts are real; how they keep us alive. Hold us up.

But she scares me, now. I don't trust her motives for choosing this Vince. And why is she avoiding my eyes and shutting me out? It can't be helped; it's just not the time to try and explain my secrets, these titbits of love, of the ring, of the mystery of Geoff and of Pittsburgh.

For now Lowie's listening for the blast of a horn outside, and when she hears it—she'll go running to Vince. This Vince, whom I already dislike. I know his type and he's not coming in. But I'm glad: I'll help her carry her luggage, and my eyes will be shutting him out.

So all I'll ever see—is a black Mercedes.

*

"Mrs. Dawson…I've got some very bad news…"

"It's Clem. Clem's dead, isn't he?"

"May I come in?"

"Why should I let *you* in? And listen to your lies?"

"I just want to explain—"

"How Clem died? I don't care how. It won't be true. You'll never tell the truth. How can you? Not when he's been killed—by *you*—by all of you. You filthy rotten traitors, you greedy…"

"Now please, Mrs. Dawson, I think you're jumping to conclusions. Clem died in the line of duty. Hundreds of other policemen were there with him. The entire Unit was called to Pittsburgh yesterday, as back-up for the disturbance caused by the strikers, over the strikebreakers. The picket lines fell, the steelworkers just went berserk—with fire-bombs, broken bottles, human barricades, the works."

"No…" Becky's voice faltered and her eyes filled with tears—but she stood rigid at the door. Indomitable. Beyond grief.

"Such a terrible tragedy…we lost four men, in all. A warehouse caught fire—"

"But Clem wouldn't go to Pittsburgh," Becky sneered. You lie. I know, you see, how he was going after those gangsters. The ones…up in the hills. Wasn't *that* the Special Mission?"

"I'm so sorry. But we were all, all of us, called away. So unexpectedly, to Pittsburgh. To control the riot."

"Not Clem. So if he's dead, he's lying up in the hills. Killed by people you know. You let it happen. Go ask Denton. He knows…how I know."

Becky was numb with rage. She glared at Clem's superior, this Trooper, and could hardly believe he was real. This Captain, whose eyes simply flickered for an instant, as if he was hit by a sudden puff of wind, or smoke. Hardly enough to ruffle a man's composure, or interrupt his line of speech.

For a moment his eyes acknowledged the force of her words, but nothing else moved. His stance at the door still steady, respectful; his face still somber and limp. No change to the sad-mouthed expression.

And his hat, held in his hands in front of his holster strap, rested in exactly the same position.

"I'm real sorry, Mrs. Dawson," he mumbled. "We all mourn, curse the injustice of our loss, but policeman risk their lives—every day—to keep the peace and uphold the law."

"Then may the Law of God take you straight to hell," Becky answered.

Before she slammed the door. Slammed it shut, right then and there. For if she hadn't—she'd have to watch the Captain wipe her spit off his face.

The ring was all, all, all. All she had left, and it fit her left forefinger; kept her sane as she closed Dibbs eyes, arranged his corpse; pulled on his boots.

But what would he say? Now, lying beyond life, with his body's shell still warm on her couch?

Becky knew it would surely be one of his quotes, a line or two from Shakespeare. Or the Bible.

"For there is no remembrance of the wise more than of the fool for ever; seeing that which now is in the days to come shall all be forgotten. And how dieth the wise man? As the fool. Ecclesiasties, Chapter Two, Verse Sixteen."

Becky read the words out loud, and sighed, and closed the book. "Ah, Dibbs," she moaned, "Where's Clem? Is he resting inside the ring, like you? Measure for Measure, I hope our poet is right, and 'Death's a great disguiser.'"

Then, holding the ring to her lips, she locked the door to the parlor and slowly climbed the stairs to wake her sons.

Chapter Seventeen

The Money

I'm pretty sure Lowie's not coming back. Things still remain in her room, but they don't belong to her. Not to Lowie, of today. The one who's chucking her past.

I guess I don't blame her, either, for not wanting to clear all of it out. That can come later, when it's easier. When enough time has passed, so it's almost unreasonable and silly to cry, or snivel, or feel so acutely reminded.

So much for keeping in touch. We can't. Not now.

Why would she want to see me, and be reminded of Geoff?

And Geoff, he's still somewhere close, I think, but he's keeping away. I suppose he knows.

It's been two weeks, and a couple of days. It drags on. And on. While I wait.

You see, I'm beginning to understand this game, and I don't want to choose. I want to love *both* Lowie and Geoff. But somehow its all got twisted and knarled, like a sailor's knot. Which loop do you loosen first? Which strand do you keep a grip?

Neither.

Rush with knots and you'll make a mistake. Better to wait for the tension to slack. Don't push, just wait till you're calm and the way out gets easy. When it's loose again, something will happen: though what might happen, I haven't a clue.

While this morning, I find, is lurching ahead toward summer. A day that's going to be sizzling hot. And since I don't have a class till the afternoon, I put on my cutoffs, grab a towel, and pack some books to lug to the Green. I need to lie on the grass. Bake in the sun. And maybe, just maybe, I'll be able to study. Or possibly finish a paper that was due last Friday.

But no. I haven't even passed through our little Oleander courtyard when I see him. Sitting quite still in the shade, shirtless and cross-legged like a stone Buddha in the gravel. Propped in this circle of gravel, under a canopy of waxy leaves drooping off the rubber plants.

With no shirt on he looks even more like a god, or a specter of Samson: the long mane of blond hair, the ravishing shoulders, muscled arms, bulge of phallus, curve of thighs, all of him pure male and built to perfection. Primed for action. But yet he's sitting so still. There's a glow in his face, but the pose is so frozen. Like a stubborn relic. A piece of stone stuck in another world—gripped to the backside of a woman.

I stop.

I'm struck, of course, by his unexpected presence and even though I've spotted him—I'm not quite convinced. Standing there gaping, not sure if what I'm staring at is really this person I know by the name of Geoff—or simply a reflection of my inner mind. Just another vivid, heart-thumping vision.

But he stands up, and moves. Suddenly I'm inches away from his skin. That's real skin, I'm thinking. And he's real—like me. So stop standing there Nina, holding your breath like a fool. Say something.

"Geoff...Hi. What are you doing?"

"Hanging around—like a stray dog." Blue acid eyes, rock hard, are keeping watch. Checking every corner. "What are you doing?"

"Going to study on campus." I hug my towel, turn my back so he can see my pack, heavy. Stuffed to the hilt with proof. "I'm heading for the lawn. My favorite spot on the Green."

"Mind if I tag along?"

He's got a T-shirt, I notice. He picks it up off the gravel and swings it over his shoulder. Jesus. I'm in such a state, I'm wishing he'd put it back on.

And I can't deny it any longer: know I'm in love and this isn't going to be easy.

"No," I manage to answer. "Of course I don't mind."

There doesn't seem to be any credibility to Lowie's story when Geoff's near. Suddenly I couldn't care less whether I see him again next week, or next year. His presence—his power—simply obliterates time. It's like he pulls you in with him, to nothing but *now*. No past, no future. Just now.

While we're lying together on the grass, and his shirt's off, his chest is broad, smooth and hairless. He's leaning over to say something. He's too close. The clock stops ticking.

In the silence I'm burning, blazing. On fire. Staring at my book where rows of black ink sizzle and vibrate in the blinding sun.

"Is she in love with him?"

The words come from his lips in one quick breath, a soft airy sound that seems to echo the she, she, she—until I realize he's stuttered it. Stumbled over the pain.

I lift my eyes from the blinding book but I don't dare look at him. There's grass. Deep, deep down between the blades I catch a glimpse of earth. The brown soil that's giving life to millions of short-lived green blades. Though I'm not surprised it's all happening again.

Is she in love with him? I'd almost forgotten the question.

"I guess so. I don't know."

"If she's in love with him, so be it," he mutters. Then he turns from me and says, "If it's true, I'll go away. Let her be."

"How can she be in love with him?" I answer. "She hasn't known him long enough."

Geoff laughs. But it's abrupt. More like a snort.

"Don't give me that," he says. "That's bullshit."

"All right, but what do you want me to say?"

"Nina, Nina—" and he suddenly grabs my neck with his hand and pulls my face to his. My eyes are moist, hidden and pressed against his throat. But my lips are shut tight, choked by a throb and pulse of Geoff's current, seeping through his skin. For a moment, his hair brushes over my cheeks as he holds me.

But just as quickly, he lets go and looks at me as if *I* should know why it all happened.

And I'm shaking my head, as if Lowie really is in love with Vince, even though I know she's not—not in the right way—and Geoff should know that too.

But is he doubting? Even I could have my doubts. You can't be sure with eyes like Lowie's. Eyes that suddenly change and shut things out. But my judgment's clouded. It feels so life and death, like an answer to my own—not Lowie's—survival. And how could Geoff trust me enough to give him a truthful answer?

Still, he's watching my face. He assumes I know. Please, Geoff, I'm thinking, don't ask me.

"Nina, what do you think? Should I let her go?"

I struggle, like I did with my dad. A few seconds, a horrific moment. Of struggle. Then, an answer I never really intended to say.

"Yes," I mumble, but still shaking my head. As if it's true and there isn't any hope. As if she's shut us both out and there's no going back.

The sweat starts to drip off my forehead, but I keep shaking my head. I don't mean to do it, but why should I give him any hope? Why me? Because I can't, not like this: wallowing in his passion, driven by selfish desire. I'm no different.

Pretending it's all for the best. So many reasons to cushion a lie.

He should know how we fall. He, more than anyone else I've ever known.

But he's forgotten: Nobody's clean.

*

Becky remembered Clem's promise of a place of their own. A homestead. Some land. Yes, she'd do anything to get out of the Valley. Take her children away—as far as possible—from the sight of downtown Greenswood, and the company of certain people. But the talk was growing, how Prohibition, at last, was to end. Some said Congress would pass an Amendment before Christmas.

But that didn't matter now. What did matter was how she could destroy Denton. Make him pay for what he'd done. After all, there were ways to make him suffer. Things could happen. An act of God: his store could catch fire. It could burn down. He could rebuild, but what if there's another fire, and so on, until he's forced to leave. Find somewhere else to spend all his money.

At first she resented Clem's stash, and why he'd kept it a secret. But with his dream to fulfill, and a family to raise—Becky's conscience gave in. She decided to follow Clem's instructions and keep the money. She'd use it to secure her revenge and force Denton out of town. There was the runner boy's family. Surely they would want to know who the murderer was and help her set fire to all Denton's stores. The arson could be made to look accidental.

Then there was Dibbs. She could help fund a home for alcoholics and the homeless.

Whatever was left would be put towards a house in the hills, and the boys' college education.

For she hadn't forgotten the fork at Bear Creek, or the rock under an oak tree to mark the spot.

She only had to dig. Yes, keep on digging, and think of those days at the farm—when the air smelled of dense pine and Clem made love to her, tucked away in the trees. And imagine a two-story clapboard house painted yellow with a porch, perched on a mountain where the birds, rabbits, and deer, all nibble the grass. Where Andrew and Ben could run through the ferns and the birch, searching for acorns and mushrooms. And she, following with her basket, would be content with her memories.

For the woods will always be there, at Evergreen Acres.

*

"You thirsty?"

Geoff's voice is hollow, and abrupt. Why does he sound so hoarse, I'm thinking. It's been hours since we last spoke.

I nod.

"Good. Let's go for a beer, yes?"

All this time I've been keeping very still. Lying there with my eyes glued to the dense rows of ink splattered in neat lines across the page. Occasionally, I choose a different page. Geoff sitting beside me with his hands moving like claws over his face. An instinctive grip: a slow wrenching to silence his prey and immobilize his writhing despair.

But it's over. He's ready to carry on.

I close the book.

"Where?"

Geoff rises. He's putting on his shirt.

"Do you have any money on you?" he mutters.

"No….do you?"

"Nope. But then I make it a point, never to have any money." He's trying to sound off-hand. "So I bet he does, doesn't he? This what's-his-name...Vince."

I ignore this, and start walking.

Fifteen or thirty blocks, and we're still walking.

We don't speak. It's too hot. We're tired and parched and I'm wondering where in L.A. we'll ever find beer that's free and quenches such an enormous thirst.

And I'm wondering, too, why Geoff makes a point of having no money. He certainly likes it, acting the part of a bum. Does he find comfort in wearing tattered clothes and never cutting his hair, which isn't exactly the norm? Does he like being teased—or more likely threatened—for sporting a pierced ear? I can only guess Geoff's IQ is too high for his own good, and he infuriates those who think having a bit of money isn't so bad. Rather necessary, it would seem, to get on in life. You've got to have a few basic things.

Maybe he resents having rich parents who are keen to help him get it all out of his system. With money. But that won't work with Geoff. When a brilliant mind is obsessed with the abyss, all the money in the world isn't going to fill it.

Not that he's told me any of this. But it could explain some of the things Lowie said. After all, it doesn't take a psychic to know if you hate money, you've got to roam. Move around and see who's there to take you in; prove there's a realm where food, drink, shelter, love and chance encounters come along and none of it revolves around the scuzz. Or what you have, or what you do. It's the biggest leap you can take, into the unknown. And I bet things happen to him a lot more than they do with me. I bet he's an expert on nutbags.

So it's not surprising, how we end up drowning our sorrows in the seediest part of town. With lots of other bums: Geoff seems to know them by name. And me, staggering along beside, the sidewalks scotching my feet, smiling at the litter—the cans and glass—that flash and glitter in the sun, until I find myself suddenly washing dishes for too few pitchers of beer in a greasy Mexican joint called Paco's.

Geoff swats at the flies and smiles at me over the table, laughing at my dismay over how I look—drenched in awe and sweat.

Until it's late and dark and we're drunk and we somehow find ourselves back in the Courtyard, where it all began. I'm not sure why he's staggered all this way by my side, or what he's thinking. Though his smile is subtle and unnerving, like a demon's.

I'm stumbling up the steel-rod stairs; I say nothing and he simply follows me in. Spellbound by the gleam in his eye, bidding me closer—he collapses on the couch. I touch him, finally, and the burning goes on, lying speechless in each other's arms.

I'm almost asleep when he gently slips inside, and rocks with his mouth, his breath, buried in my hair. Are we making love? For I'm thinking this feels like death making love, an oblivious falling into bliss, and I'm as open as the sky; my coming is limitless. But Geoff still lives on: in shudders and writhes, gripping his lust with leg muscles taunt, hands still tracing the skin round my eyes to show his intent: he wants it to happen again.

And it stays. He's pulling me up, tossing our clothes aside; we stand naked. In the sparse light of dawn I see tiny jewels in his eyes—like sapphires—as he moves to caress my legs, his fingers taking hold there, there, there, and he's lifting me up. I whimper, sob, dissolve in his hands: a passion so strong he clenches me tight, gritting his teeth to whisper: "Feel it, Nina. We *are* the void."

*

I am Becky.

Sitting under a big oak tree, with many long large twisty branches interwoven above, the bark, brown, hard and old, carved with layers and lines and bumps and holes of time, bugs crawling on the bark, moss crawling on the roots, the ground soft, clumpy, grassy, the air cool, clear, crisp, surrounding the rolling fields, the banks of the river, the rocks and pines, the hills vivid, glowing, etched against the blue, clear sky, crystal clouds, distant blackbirds flapping, fleeting, gone, the treetops pointing up the hills, over the horizon, the breeze blowing, ruffling the long, tall weeds, grass, and the clustered strands of my hair.

Thinking under a big oak tree, here, now, the hills, the fields, the grass, trees, birds, flying high, gliding through the good, quiet country, here, forever here, all around this oak tree, strong, solitary, forever standing, feeling, seeing, here, now, before, past, future, always, the branches long, gnarled, reaching, holding the open sky, vast, empty, endless blue with birds and clouds and winds of time, of beauty, calm, the feeling here, mingling through the far-reaching hills, heading home to the mountains, trees, fields, blankets of grass, farms, barns, and the muddy tracks of a wagon.

A cow.

Watching, grazing, lazy, munching, lifting its nose, wondering, sniffing, checking, listening to the muffled sobbing, a human huddling, rocking, shaking, lying under a big oak tree, growing silent, small, lost, limp, a cause for chewing, flies buzzing, tail flicking, fur burly, brown, dusty, raw.

God.

Comforting, lifting me, a woman, rising, sighing, carrying a basket, slowly moving from under the big oak tree.

Bugs.

Waiting…then returning.

Climbing and crawling, over the matted spot of grass.

Chapter Eighteen

The Ring

A scraping noise wakes me. The chinking of keys in the lock. I know it's the front door.

Lowie.

My heart sinks like a lead ball down a mineshaft, wham, boom, boom boom. My. God. She's. Back.

Right-now-this-minute.

No. No.

Yes.

Just like that. I hit bottom, and freeze. Squeeze my eyes shut, as the footsteps come closer.

And stop.

A deep silence. I can feel her eyes, blinking in disbelief, right over us. The two of us, nestled in the couch like a pair of fledglings, recently fed and now sleeping—so still, and oblivious to the world.

If only we'd moved to my bed last night, I'm thinking, but the couch seemed so neutral. Our lot. A middle space.

Eyes still closed, mind racing, out in the open on the couch, or half-hidden in my room…fuck…what's the difference?

While nothing else happens.

Geoff, he really sleeps: hair tangled in mine, limbs tossed over my body like a misspent blanket, while I pretend I'm not really me.

No, it can't be Nina who's causing this nasty scene. It's fate, and fate deals like the devil: plays the odds with loaded dice.

What should I do?

I can't do a thing.

Nor can she.

But when the front door slams, Geoff instantly wakes up.

"What was that?" he mumbles.

"I don't believe it."

"What…?" His arm moves away as I wrestle to get free. "No—it wasn't—?"

I nod. And too late, too late, to be jumping up and bursting into tears.

Slowly, Geoff follows my own clumsy moves to dress; stone-faced, he hands me a tissue and slips away, to God knows where.

But he's passed the alley behind the courtyard.

I can hear the rubbish bins crashing; a succession of slams, each followed by an explosive spray of broken glass.

The sound scares me. Hushes my own feeble sobs.

He'll hate me now, I'm thinking. And Lowie. That's it. You asked for it, Nina, so you better get a grip. Calm down. Think. Think of what you can do. Because this time, you can't just sit still and wait.

*

It's three o'clock in the afternoon, and I haven't moved. Geoff hasn't come back, and I'm beginning to wonder if I haven't completely misjudged the entire situation: mistaken the motives of us all, in fact. I mean, what makes me so sure I really know the real Lowie, or Geoff? What if they're both just using me, like a pawn being played as a trick, forcing the play into checkmate?

And what if I'm fooling myself into thinking I'm in the middle of a nutbag—when all it is, is a damn good fuck? Geoff could be toying with my emotions, just taking advantage, to get at Lowie. I mean, why not? I've got no real proof he isn't. While Lowie lets him do it, just to keep things where she wants them. With her on top.

But then I think no, the feeling can't be faked. My instincts have never failed me yet. The nutbag comes and goes, but it never fools. It's the people that do.

However. Geoff's in love, and hopelessly so, with Lowie. He might be tempted to use me just the same. Just as I've been tempted to use my own selfish means to keep him hanging around.

No matter what, it's become one big awful, guilt-ridden mess and I don't want to be part of it—not any more.

*

I find Lowie in the Gallery, of course. The one in Malibu.

It's a clinical-looking place, with white walls and pedestals, trimmed in chrome. A few potted palms. Clean as a whistle, and quieter than a library.

She's alone, sitting behind a desk in the corner, flipping through the pages of a glossy folder.

She looks up when the bell tinkles, and her face doesn't change much when she sees me. Her cheeks flush slightly pink, but her composure is controlled.

I'm relieved.

But it's a long, grueling walk—those few feet—to get closer.

She doesn't move. Safer, I suppose, keeping the solid desk between us.

"Lowie…."

"—I'd like to come and collect the rest of my things," she cuts in, to make it easier. "And I'll give you back the keys. That's only fair, as I don't intend to pay the last month's rent."

"If that's what you want," I answer, in a voice just as weak and shaky as hers.

"Shall we say, about ten tomorrow morning?"

"I'll be in class."

"That doesn't matter, does it? I won't take anything that isn't mine."

"But we need to talk," I add. "Lowie, please."

Her eyes challenge me to go on. Thank goodness, I'm thinking, she's trying to be fair.

"I'm not mad at—you—," Lowie murmurs. "None of this is purely your fault. So don't apologize, OK?"

"I didn't mean for it to happen," I insist. "I was only trying to be a friend…"

She smiles, with that half-evil, cynical, quirky lift in her corner lip.

"Nina, listen. After all, if the two of us are friends, maybe I should tell you. If he hasn't."

"Tell me what?"

She hesitates, as if to emphasize the point, and repeats, "I assume he hasn't told you, has he?"

I shake my head. My heart's pounding even harder now, like a wind-up toy gone berserk. Thumping madly in all directions. All sorts of possibilities pop into…

"I think you should know—Geoff—he—prefers men," Lowie finally stammers. "He'll deny it, but you best know what you're getting into. I'm only mentioning it since you're so—inexperienced—and—new at—his kind of thing."

"I don't understand what you mean," I reply.

"Look. Just go see a doctor," Lowie says. "Make sure you get checked for venereal disease. I did. Geoff advised me to, which was considerate of him, don't you think? He admits he probably picked it up during one of his trips to San Francisco. These buddies of his…or whoever. Like I said before, he tends to wander and then disappear, and it usually involves sex with men, women, all of them strangers."

Like me, I'm thinking. And he's passing it on to me.

Yet I feel no disgust, or outrage. Maybe I'm in a state of shock. Or denial.

"Oh," I reply. Just Oh.

Lowie, apparently expecting this response, doesn't bother to press further.

"Just thought you should know," she says.

I nod. She's looking down at the folder and creasing the edge of the page.

"You'll take my advice, then."

"Yes."

I turn, and leave her there, as Vince (it must be him) comes prancing in with a take-away, and waits for me to pass, politely holding the door.

While I notice how he glances down, checking the size of my breasts: expecting me to blush. Waver. And acknowledge how good he looks.

Which for Lowie's sake, I do.

*

I'm glad he hasn't appeared again. No, I really am. Because these last two weeks were hard enough as it was—taking finals and handing in four papers. Which I did, much to my surprise. But of course it got easier, once I decided to give up the nutbag thing for good. Call it quits and admit I'd been wrong. Go back to being normal again.

And my dad will be happy. He won't be disappointed.

I'm thinking this as I'm walking back to the apartment, after standing around the Main Campus Building for hours—part of the graduation rehearsal. It's a sunny day and I'm looking forward to going to a party tonight. Like I used to do.

So. Nobody's clean, and you have to draw the line somewhere.

At first I kept going back to the Green, hoping. But no Geoff. Then I kept peeking out the apartment window, checking out the plants, down in the Courtyard. No Geoff there either. He'd vanished, like I expected him to—if what Lowie said was all there was to it. Well, she was right.

As far as the curtain goes, I've been keeping it closed. Which doesn't bother me much either, because I never want to know what really happened to Clem. I'd rather leave them both forever there, under the Oak tree, where everything merges together, and life simply carries on.

Funny, though, isn't it? I'm climbing the stairs to the apartment, rational as can be, and the next minute I'm standing at the front door, when suddenly the last two weeks slide right down the drain.

I'm staring at something sticking under the mat.

It's small and oblong, and I when I pick it up, I realize it's a piece of gum.

*

Geoff is whistling softly under his breath as we walk. He's got a strange gleam in his eye, as if he's leading me, with great amusement, into one of his favorite pranks.

I mean, he keeps smiling and glancing at me, checking. But I'm hooked on the nutbag again, keen as ever. He doesn't need to check, but he's teasing—with that look—reminding me I might be capable of changing my mind. Yes, making sure with a smile so sharp and mischievous I want to grab his face…and consume eyes, nose, cheeks, lips, jaw, everything. Every inch of that expression which so effortlessly—and almost cruelly—plays upon my deepest desires.

And to make it even worse, he takes my hand. His hand in mine: a connection I can hardly endure, because my nerve-endings are already obliterated by this other sensation. Well beyond.

We hitchhiked to get here. I woke up at ten, with this telltale knock on the door, and Geoff was waiting outside. He said I looked like I needed a wander.

Well.

I think I'm confused as hell over his intentions, but I'm beginning to get the hang of his "wanders." You can end up walking aimlessly for miles. This time we've ambled clean out of L.A. so I'm glad we cheated and used a car.

It can't be helped. I mean, Jesus. Even now, I'll follow him anywhere.

Though we're not that far. Twenty or thirty miles up the Pacific Coast.

"Is there something I should know?" I finally ask.

We're cutting through a parking lot. It's empty.

Off to one side, a narrow lane disappears down a canyon, and the sign says PRIVATE.

It feels like a long time since that day. When I went searching for Lowie and she told me those things in the Gallery. And those finals to take, which I took, though I haven't a clue if I actually passed.

"That sounds ominous. What are you so anxious to know?" Geoff answers, catching my tone of suspicion.

"If you've given me the clap?" That's what I should feel compelled to say—but I don't.

Instead, I mumble "Oh, nothing." But suddenly I halt, forcing Geoff to halt. "No. I've got to tell you, I've seen Lowie," I confess. "Since that morning."

"So have I," Geoff adds.

"When?"

"Last week."

"And?"

"I snapped. Broke. Slobbered and sobbed like a tortured prisoner. She knows she's killing me by marrying this jerk. Her nice-man Vince, her way of revenge. But she also knows—stipulations and vows are something Geoff can't keep."

"Such as being faithful?"

"Love never deceives!" Geoff exclaims. "Real love never chooses between itself. There isn't a need for it, is there? But we who do the loving, we measure and choose. Lovers deceive, it's true. But what can you say, Nina, of passion divine? Are we meant to limit its power to lift, to touch? Close our eyes, our hearts, and ignore the continuous message? Or pretend to confine it?"

I don't answer. Just smile, because I can't disagree. Though how we might work it out with all our human frailties, I'm not sure.

"But when we love, we shouldn't be hurting other people," I hasten to say.

"Deceit, ego and pride—they can hurt," Geoff replies. "But not love: not the kind we're talking about."

With that, he's off walking again, and I follow him down the lane—expecting, if not the security police, at least a few angry dogs.

Especially this time of night.

"I'd like to know what we're doing now—" I mutter as he gropes to unhinge a gate.

"I want to show you something," he says, as we pass through the gate, and our feet hit sand.

He stops to kick off his shoes.

"On the beach?" I ask, following suit and hardly able to contain my—curiosity—for much longer.

"I picked here, but it doesn't have to be here. The beach will do. And when we find the place—we'll know."

So I'm right: he's definitely got something in mind.

It's strange, too, because I'm not feeling tired. It's taken all day to get this far, but I'm alert as an owl at midnight. It must be close to that hour, because nobody's here. We're completely alone on this sidetrack stretch of beach. Just us, tramping across the sand. Listening to the sound of the waves breaking in the gentle swell of darkness. The waves, not distant but obscure. No moon.

"Come on…" He smiles and takes my hand again, and I suddenly feel peculiar. The torment eases. The touch of his skin feels cool—almost bloodless—as I dig my toes into the sand and turn to admire the beach through the evening's black veil.

The air and sea smell saltier and the tinge of dank seaweed tickles my nose. The lights from the oilrigs blink up at the stars, while the gentle swell of the incoming tide lulls the shore with its whoosh, whoosh and soft sighing plash as it sinks and creeps down through the sand; up and down, back and forth…so fluid, so softly, softly, rocking…

"Do you feel the spirit?" Geoff asks quietly, squeezing my hand. "It's good the sea is calm. No breeze, no moon."

"Yes," I say, taking a deep breath, because I'm completely sober. We're both sober, for a change. No booze, no pot, no pills. And yet I'm finding it hard to believe—so on the brink as I am—of losing my composure. My trusty sober foothold.

But Geoff seems to know, and he pauses to study my face.

"Are you all right?" His voice sounds weird, more like music: "You know what I'm talking about, don't you?" The words seem to ring in my ears from a faraway place. "Nina. Don't be afraid."

But yes, I'm thinking, I am a little bit afraid.

What's happening to his voice? Why does he sound so different? While his face, it's almost transforming: skin rising like a mist, breathing out into the air…

"What am I on?" I ask.

"Nothing," Geoff sings. "Now, think. When would I have slipped you something without your knowing?"

I think. I want to find a how, or a when—but I can't.

"Trust me," Geoff insists, his features now a flux of changing light, like rainbow-coral currents swirling to fill the inner pockets and jagged gaps of a rocky cove.

I almost laugh: he's coming alive with a kind of glow that makes me think of a sorcerer. And he wants me to trust what I see? How does he know I'll believe?

"I'm not on anything," I whisper.

"That's so—and better," he replies. While the lines of his face sway in waves, lips float apart.

I squint, and focus, but it doesn't change the brightness of his eyes, all intricate rays of light, twitching and coiling like electric snakes.

He lets go of my hand, and in shock I walk on; follow close as he ambles and searches; inspects the cliffs as they become visible in the darkness ahead.

"Here," he suddenly says, "near these cliffs around the bend." A reverent tone. As if he assumes I'll understand.

But I don't, not until we get there and I begin to feel a tingling in my head, and a soft, tantalizing ringing in my ears, which seems to bounce off the rocks and whir in front of my face. I'm feeling dizzy. The tingling and ringing is making me stagger. I resist moving any further.

"Wait! Don't let go of my hand," Geoff commands. He grabs it and pulls me closer toward the inner recess of the cliffs. I know it can't be, but it sounds like's he's shouting. Even so I can hardly hear him, over the din in my head. Or is it all around me? An amazing whirling intensity, like unseen bats let loose in the dark.

"Don't be afraid," Geoff reminds me. "Keep hold of my hand—don't let go. No matter what."

Above us in the darkness, the steep wall of the cliff leans toward us like an enormous cupped hand, silhouetted in black. A black blacker than the night air.

No wonder I'm scared, and still Geoff pulls me along; never letting go of my hand; sitting me down.

We're both anchored in the sand, in the middle, like two rocks marking a center.

"Do you see?" Geoff finally mutters, because there's no breeze, no cold, nothing but the cliff's edge that is moving into an outline. A circle, enfolding us both in a circular shape. The shadows vibrating: a haunting, thrilling host of nameless things fly about us in the empty space. And they keep growing. These specs like spirits, crazy and dancing and too fast to catch, calling out to us in high-pitched strains as they flit past, swooping and diving like swifts.

I see, but am I convinced?

While Geoff's face, fluid and luminous, looms closer. Forcing me to look again, into his eyes. Out of the darkness, glimmering. Breath-taking.

"Nina, speak…let your true self speak," he finally commands.

My head is spinning. I can feel the grip of Geoff's hand, but now I'm tempted to let go. Leave mind and body behind, let the spirits whisk me away….

"Speak!" Geoff repeats.

I obey, but it takes such an effort. And when I do open my mouth, something wordless comes out: it doesn't sound like a word. It's more like an echo, a stream of notes from a two-syllable song coming from a hundred mouths.

I say "Nina" and the syllables erupt from my lips and burst like a fountain, a chorus—of immeasurable sound. Out, out, and everywhere; caught on the wings of the screaming spirits, and carried across the ocean, and scattered over the black void beyond the horizon.

The circle is broken. Gradually the vibration settles, and I hear nothing but the sound of the waves.

*

"Is it sapphire?"

Geoff's bending down, inspecting the flower on my finger.

He's noticed the ring.

Well.

It's enough just to hear him ask. I mean, we're saying goodbye and I realize.

It's the ring. The last thing.

"Yes," I reply. "It's sapphire. My grandmother's ring. You see, my grandmother had this little ritual..."

"No—" Geoff shakes his head. He sees the tears forming in my eyes, and doesn't want me to start. Instead, he kisses the ring on my hand, and that's how we'll part.

The bus is ready, people are impatient, behind.

"I'll tell you about it someday..."

"I won't write—"

"I know. But Geoff—"

"I can't promise we'll meet again."

"No! Don't say that! I mean, I can't imagine...I'll never see you again. And who else is there? How can I stand it without you?"

"You trust me, yes?"

I nod.

"Just remember, then. Remember the beach. You have it all, Nina. You can stand anything."

"But what...happens now?"

"Don't forget, but don't tell a soul what you saw. If you tell, no one will believe it."

"No one?"

"You know as well as I do, Nina. When you least expect it, you'll find your next bum. And he'll recognize you at once. Wait for him, damn it. Don't sing your name on the beach with anyone else."

"And Lowie?"

"You'll be there for her, yes?"

I nod. I think I will, even though I've been to the doctor and the tests came out clean. I guess we both could use a bit of forgiving.

"*Tempus Fugit.*" His smile twists into that familiar subtle smirk, as he touches my cheek and turns away. Boards the bus. Disappears forever.

He's leaving, I'm thinking. He really is. But I guess I'm beginning to accept—how scuzz always covers a nutbag.

Staring at the back of his battered green T-shirt, and the sun-bleached ponytail swishing off his shoulders, I don't even attempt to wave as he hops up the steps. Turns out of sight.

While just as abruptly I'm walking away, and not looking back, because I know there's no need. Not when I've solved the mystery of the ring, and Becky's left the stage open to the future.

For it's always there, and I get the feeling when I close my eyes and pull back the curtain, I'll be seeing blond hair.

And blue eyes.

About the Author

Lisa Ammerman is an American (age 45, BA in English) who spent a number of years living in England (Nottingham), and is a published writer of short stories. Her short stories and articles have appeared in *My Weekly*, *People's Friend*, *The Lady*, and *Amateur Gardener*. On the literary side, two stories have been published in Small Press Publications; others have been shortlisted in UK fiction competitions such as World Wide Writers. *Love in a Nutbag* is her second novel.